Stargazing

Stargazing

Glimpses of a Life More Twinkly

Lynne O'Sullivan

Matador
9 Priory Business Park
Kibworth Beauchamp
Leicestershire LE8 0RX, UK
Tel: (+44) 116 279 2299
Fax: (+44) 116 279 2277
Email: books@troubador.co.uk
Web: www.troubador.co.uk/matador

ISBN 978 1780884 240

British Library Cataloguing in Publication Data.
A catalogue record for this book is available from the British Library.

Typeset in 12pt Garamond by Troubador Publishing Ltd, Leicester, UK

Matador is an imprint of Troubador Publishing Ltd

Printed and bound in the UK by TJ International, Padstow, Cornwall

Cover design by Lynne O'Sullivan

PART ONE

THE DREAMER

Drama has always seemed to follow me whether I've asked for it or not. A summer storm raged as I entered the world in the early hours of an August morning, my arrival having been provoked by a dish of sprats at Sunday tea. My grandmother hurried to the phone box across Newtown green for the ambulance, while my mother sat in the white pebble dashed house wondering what lay in store.

Like Oliver Twist, you could say that I was born in a workhouse, Willesborough Hospital having once been the East Ashford Union refuge for the poor and disparate. During the time of the workhouse, a distant ancestor, one Thomas Spice, had been an inmate. In 1881 conditions there were hopefully not as bleak as in other establishments in the UK. In any event, eighty year old Thomas did not last more than a year in the place before he passed away.

Spice was my mother's maiden name. Her family hailed from Kennington, another Ashford suburb. Before that they were found at Romney Marsh from where it's been suggested that they were smugglers who dealt in spices and other goods. Another possibility is that they came from northern France and the name is a derivative of 'Epicier' or grocer.

My distant grandfather, Charles (1711-1790) was at one time warden at Kennington Church and is buried close beside it. Charles lived through the reigns of three King George's, (the last one being the subject of the famous play, *The Madness of King George III*). When his wife Mary died aged fifty-seven, Charles married again, this time to Catherine, thirty-five years his junior. Going a bit Michael Douglas he erred on the side of caution and specified in his will that Cath should inherit his 'furniture, linen, plate and china' until she re-married. Presumably after that, she had to buy her own pots and pans.

Further back, during the reign of Elizabeth I, one Robert Spyce owned property at Henwood and in the town's Middle Row. In his will of 1550, Robert provided for his four children, Richard, John, Margaret and Julie Ann. The boys got his property, the girls a few shillings each. By the 1800s the estate was lost, either through high taxes or at the gambling tables, who knows? In any case my Spice ancestors were then working on the land rather than owning any of it themselves.

When I was a kid, Middle Row was home to Rabson's toy shop, an Aladdin's cave of wonderful things. The door opened to rows of little dogs on wheels, doll's prams and cots. Cuddly teddies of all sizes sat along the shelves with brightly dressed gollies, rag dolls, gorgeous bride dolls and clowns in satin outfits. (These were always a bit cheaper than regular dolls as you couldn't take their clothes off).

Beneath the glass counter there were cowboys,

redskins and cavalry. A slide-out drawer contained bags of 'Jacks' coloured silver and gold. There were swirly-patterned rubber balls for the endless games of 'Two-ball' along with 'Fuzzy Felt' and 'Beetle Drives', jigsaws and compendiums of games.

Several of my ancestors were married at the parish church nearby, among them my great-aunt Ethel, whose story would surely make a good film or TV drama on its own. Frail from bouts of tuberculosis which dogged her life, Ethel didn't marry until she was thirty-four and then to a widower twenty years her senior. From her wedding photograph, Ethel's marriage to Frank Pellatt looks a rather austere occasion. Ethel in her dainty outfit and cloche hat is flanked by her brother Sid and sister Rose, with their father, John Spice standing behind them on the step. (Unfortunately, this step has been a casualty during the recent conversion of part of the church into an arts centre). My great-grandfather sports a full moustache and a serious expression despite having a reputation for his jolly nature. This was probably due to everyone being on their best behaviour in front of a camera in those days and not wanting to waste their money or the photographer's time. John and Rose were witnesses to the wedding, but when John's own father, Stephen Spice had married Mary Howe at Kennington Church in 1861, both bride and groom signed the register with a cross, indicating that neither could read nor write.

Ethel and Frank were to spend merely four years together in their home in Faversham Road. In 1934 when she was thirty-eight, Ethel went into Ashford Hospital to give birth to baby. She was once again addled with tuberculosis and despite undergoing a caesarian section, the effort proved too much for her frail constitution, so that Frank returned to the little end cottage alone.

In a photograph taken in their back yard in Kennington, my great-grandparents, John and Sarah Spice sit with their daughters Ethel and Rose, sons Sid (with his wife Connie), Percy James (my grandfather) and family friend 'Spud'. My ancestors look out across the years. I know their names, the dates of their births, their marriages, when they died and how. It's weird to think that someone in the future might one day be looking at old photographs of me and my family. Hopefully, we won't turn out to be as doomed as these relatives who seemed to go from one tragedy to another.

In the photograph, my great-grandmother was sixty-two, but appears far older due to her life being full of hard work and worry. Her main concern may well have been the tuberculosis affecting her children. The disease was rife in Kent from the late 1800s to the 1930s. Ethel and her brother Sid fell victim before penicillin became available as a treatment. Both spent time in Kennington's Grosvenor Sanatorium where sufferers resided during bouts of the disease.

Ethel's brother, my great-uncle Sid died three years after the photograph was taken, aged thirty. The disease had spread into his foot which eventually had to be removed. The shock of this added to the once athletic

Sid's despair, and he passed away soon after the amputation. His brother Percy James, my grandfather was to die of asbestos poisoning after working with the stuff in the railway factory before it was known to be lethal.

By all accounts, Sarah Spice was a strong and down to earth lady, but having been widowed five years before and with three of her children dead from tuberculosis, it wasn't surprising that she ended up taking her own life one dark December day in 1946 at her Kennington home.

Out of all of the people in the photograph, 'Spud' was the only one I ever got to meet, although he was by then very old. He would give half crowns to my sister Mo and I when we were children if we saw him in the street. The once the handsome lad pictured with our family, was just a friendly old man with a kindly smile.

Almost opposite the door to the Parish church where Ethel's wedding photograph was taken, is Ashford's quaint museum. It was built by Sir Norton Knatchbull in 1635 as a grammar school for boys. The young tykes' graffiti can still be seen carved into the wainscoting and the niches where their books were placed are still there. Also on show is the seat that belonged to the headmaster himself. In the picture a group of boys play outside the building.

A stone's throw from Middle Row is what was once Ashford's Odeon picture house. It's here, during the

Saturday morning picture club that I first got bitten by the 'acting bug'. The place would be packed with kids and the noise deafening as *The Lone Ranger* and Tonto flickered across our faces. The vague smell of tobacco would hang in the air from the previous night's audience. It was quite all right to smoke in cinemas back then in the mid 60s. There were even little ashtrays attached to the backs of seats for the purpose. Surprisingly, there were very few reported incidents of cinemas and theatres burning to the ground. Health and safety didn't apply as much in 1965 as plain common sense. The morning's proceedings would open with the usual song to which we'd sing along at the tops of our voices...

We come along, on Saturday morning, greeting everybody with a smile!
We come along on Saturday morning, knowing it's well worthwhile!
As members of the Cinema Club we all intend to be
Good citizens when we grow up and members of the free!
We come along on Saturday morn-ing (this bit quite high)
Ga-reeting everybody with a smile, smile, SMILE! (huge)
Ga-reeting everybody with a SMILE!

The song was rounded off by a cartoon of a grinning man. His head gradually expanded to the size of the screen on the word 'Smile!' so you found yourself smiling whether you wanted to or not. There was usually a 'scary' film but they only showed a bit of this at a time so if you missed a week you literally lost the plot. Once the film was *The Uninvited*, set in Cornwall, directed by Lewis Allen in 1944, which involved some curtains billowing out and a lamp moving on its own. My brother and I were used to stronger stuff, like *Mystery and Imagination*, a series of spooky Victorian plays televised on Saturday evenings. Through one of our father's old sweaters we'd watch the likes of M.R. James's *Lost Hearts*, *Room 13* and *The Tractate Middoth*. Edgar Allen Poe's *Fall of the House of Usher* had us putting off going to the loo as long as possible in case something dead, or even undead, lurked beneath the stairs near the gas meter.

After the show we'd join the hoards emptying out into the high street. If we decided to spend our bus fare on sweets we would walk home along Newtown Road, past what was once known as 'The Cold Blow', a section of field skirted by the ominous 'Black Path'. This has been built over to form the roundabout adjacent to what is now the Outlet Centre. The loss of this dimly-lit walkway is a rare example of the new replacing the old to good effect, as the path had a sinister reputation. While by day it was a short cut through to South Ashford with the rattle of trains passing over the bridge, by night it was a lonely walk.

In August 1944, a fifteen year old girl was murdered in the adjacent field. Her body was discovered the following morning by a railwayman passing over the bridge. The two American servicemen responsible were court-martialled in what was once the Town Hall on the island of shops in the high street. In an upstairs room, which was later to become a hairdressers, both were found guilty and a few months later executed at Shepton Mallet prison by Britain's last hangman, Albert Pierrepont, portrayed in the 2005 film about his life by Timothy Spall. The event must have shattered the local community, despite the fact that it was wartime and everyday life already affected to a greater degree.

If we took the bus home from the pictures, the conductor would twist the dial on the ticket machine and give us our buff coloured tickets printed with 'East Kent Bus Company'. The upper deck was full of smoke and chatter and the floor littered with dog ends. Kids argued that the 'scary' film was an 'X' but of course, it wasn't. You had to be eighteen to see an X-film and even then could be asked for your birth certificate as proof. Back then most of us looked like kids until we were about twenty-five.

Our stop was the last one – a pull-in at the bottom of Hunter Avenue next to the toilets and opposite the chip shop. The buses always parked there for a while and the drivers would wander out for a smoke or to use the loo. I would dawdle up Twelve Acres, our street, still thinking about the movie, wondering how you got to be in films and have your face on a poster.

Mrs Walter, the drama teacher at my school was once an actress. She wore a net of tiny beads over her hair and was very elegant.

When I asked her about acting she said it was a tough

profession calling for hard work, determination, and a great deal of luck. In the meantime, she suggested I take the English Speaking Board exam. Thinking there might be some connection with this and getting to Hollywood, I readily agreed.

On the day of the exam, Mrs Walter sat nearby, smiling encouragingly while I recited *The Sea* by James Reeves.

"The Sea is a hungry dog, giant and grey..."

I tried to keep in mind everything Mrs Walter had taught me, like remembering to stand up straight and project my voice until I became the 'rolling sea itself'. I thought of the sea at Hythe which really was grey and rolled quite a bit in the winter when we saw it from our dad's car. As for the 'hungry dogs' – well, they could be me and my siblings on the pebbles there in summer, yelping around the picnic bag while my mother dished out sandwiches.

"It rolls on the beach all day..."

That would be me and my friend Chris lying on our towels trying to get a tan minus any sun cream.

The Speaking Board exam was conducted by veteran actress and theatre director, Esme Church. I could have no idea at twelve years old that the elderly lady seated in front of me in a tweed suit and laced-up shoes was at one time head of the Old Vic, that she had worked with the likes of Sir Michael Redgrave and Dame Edith Evans, or that she entertained British troops with concert parties in France during the First World War. This wouldn't have meant very much to me even if the information had been imparted. I was born eight years after the Second World War ended and only knew what my mother had told me of life in war-affected Ashford – the rationing and nightly air raids. When I was younger, the monument to 'our glorious dead' was merely a distraction while passing through the memorial gardens on the way to town. I'd let go of the pram and skip up the stone step to run a finger over the names of the fallen, G (George) E Spice, a distant relative, among them. In November, a wreath of poppies would be placed against the cold wet stone in bright scarlet or crimson but always red – red as blood.

I waited for a reaction from Miss Church about *The Sea*.

"Continue," she said sleepily, her eyes closed, her head on one side, spectacles dangling on a chain.

I launched into *Something Told the Wild Geese*, by Rachel Field, imagining myself a wild goose high in the sky, flying off for the winter.

When I'd finished flying, Miss Church eventually opened her eyes and looked surprised to find me standing before her instead of a battalion of cheering soldiers including George E. perhaps.

"Well done," she said. "Very good projection."

She signed my certificate and called out "Next."

Soon after this, Mrs Walter gave me the role of the princess in *The Princess and the Woodcutter*, the original princess having gone down with measles. The role involved kissing a girl called Patricia, who played the woodcutter, on the lips. I didn't really want to and it was the only drawback in what was otherwise a thrilling opportunity. When we did it in rehearsal, Patricia gave me a funny old look, like it was all my idea.

"You have to be prepared for anything in the theatre, darlings," Mrs Walter assured us. "Just get on with it."

On the afternoon of the show I stood trembling behind the rigged up curtain. My great-aunt May played Lady Macbeth in her school's production around 1924. In a photograph, she wears a nightdress, probably freshly laundered by my great-grandmother for the occasion. For the princess, my costume was the bridesmaid's dress I wore for the girl next door's wedding and a coronet my mother made from kitchen foil. I tried to ignore the terrifying sound of people taking their seats and concentrated on walking through a forest encountering a handsome woodcutter. I didn't get off to a very good start, when the girl doing stage management pulled the curtain back too far completely blowing my cover before the show had even begun. I yanked it back quickly, but not before my little sister spotted me and yelled out "'Nin!'."

It all went OK and met with the resounding applause you might expect from an audience full of mums. I was a star for the afternoon but the poster in the Odeon foyer still seemed a long way off.

*The Spice family in the
back yard in
Faversham Road
around 1928*

The Will of Robert Spyce 1550

Robert Spyce of Ashford, Yeoman - 21 June 1550

To my son, Richard, my tenement at Henwood in Willesborough with all lands thereto late bought from Robert Bargar, when Richard is 20 and to his heirs. If he die without lawful issue to John, my son, and his lawful issue.

To my son, Richard, my little tenement in Ashford adjoining upon the churchyard, and to his heirs for ever. Also my house and shop with a parcel of ground called "Little Gable" which shop Robert Cheesman now occupies and held at the will of the lord (of the manor) according to the custom of the manor.

To my son, John, the house I now dwell in with all my freehold to same, and to his heirs for ever. Also all copy-hold ground which I hold according to the custom of the manor; and my house that Thomas Basenet dwells in. Robert, son of John Spyce, all lands bought for Richard Tylden of Benynden being in Westwell, and to his heirs for ever.

July Ann, my daughter, have £6-13-4d

Margaret, my daughter, £6-13-4d

Executors - my sons, Richard and John, probate, 20 June 1552

16

Students outside
the boys'
grammar school,
Ashford
churchyard in the
1600s.

Ashford High Street 1965 – (Copyright The Francis Frith Collection). 'Murderer's Row', starring Dean Martin plays at the Odeon.

17

The War Memorial, Ashford 1960 — (Copyright The Francis Frith Collection)

Great Auntie May
as 'Lady M'
around 1924.

The Young Esme Church

Willesborough Hospital (once the workhouse)

The Grosvenor
Sanitorium,
Kennington -
(Copyright The
Francis Frith
Collection).

Sister Act

Of all the nuns at the convent school that I attended from age eleven to thirteen, I liked Sister Pius the best. She's wasn't very old for a start, probably in her early twenties. Like the other nuns, she came from Ireland. If she found anything funny she would laugh, then cover her mouth with her hand as if she was doing something she shouldn't.

Sister Pius always started a lesson with a prayer about being strong. "*To give and not to count the cost, to toil and not to seek for rest...'.*" We were supposed to have our eyes closed throughout this, but I couldn't help peeping at Sister Pius standing there all by herself praying. I'd wonder what her hair was like, whether she's had it all cut off like nuns are supposed to do. She had the sort of complexion that in civilian life would never need make-up – fresh and rosy. I imagined her in another existence, out walking in the wild Irish countryside with a husband and a couple of kids in tow, her hair blowing in the wind.

Sister Pius took the Latin and needlework lessons. One afternoon I accompanied her into the nuns' house to get material from a cupboard on the landing. The staircase smelled of polish and the floors were shiny. It was early afternoon but the place was dark and quiet as if the house itself was deep in prayer. I wondered which room belonged to Sister Pius. I took the bolts of material that she handed me and followed her back downstairs. I wondered if the nuns had a TV and if so, what sort of programmes they watched, but we passed out of the house through the kitchen without so much as a radio in sight.

If you were stuck with whatever you were making in the needlework class, Sister Pius would take your sewing into her pale hands, carefully unpick the stitches, re-thread the needle and show you where you'd gone wrong. She certainly didn't need to pray for patience, already having tons of it. We often asked her questions about where she came from in Ireland and what she thought of the latest fashions, but she always skilfully changed the subject back to needlework or Our Lord or the Blessed Virgin.

One afternoon at the start of Latin and after her opening prayer was finished, Sister Pius launched straight into conjugating the verb 'amare' – to love. My friend Winnie and I were giggling our heads off as usual. When Winnie laughed she found it impossible to stop. The laughter would take her over completely like a fit. We were taking dancing lessons around that time, every Thursday evening at Mrs Ridley's academy in Magazine Road. Win's mother kept her on a tight leash and dancing was about the only thing she approved of us doing together. Mrs Ridley's dance studio was mirrored on one side making it difficult for Winnie and I to escape each other's grinning faces as we took turns sweeping around the room clinging on to our teacher. The worst times for giggling were when we had to dance together.

"Feet!" Mrs Ridley would yell as we trod on each other's toes tango-ing to *The Isle of Capri*. Winnie laughed until tears ran down her face and would have to either disappear out of the room to the toilet or squat in a corner shaking as she pretended to adjust her shoe.

So here we were in Latin sniggering about the previous evening's lesson and words in the textbook like 'Annus' and 'Puella,' when Sister Pius moved by our desk chanting *"Amo, Amas, Amat..."*. She glanced down at our exercise books with a frown. Perhaps she'd never heard of Scott Walker or the Monkees whose names were scrawled over them in biro. I imagined her deep in prayer in the quiet house while we watched *Top of the Pops* on Thursday evenings and felt quite sorry for her. She seemed so young to be missing out on everything.

Through the window I caught sight of Sister Mary, the oldest member of the Order, approaching along one of the pathways. Sister Mary didn't have much to do except wander about checking on things. She would often interrupt a lesson to impart some vital piece of information to the teacher, her whiskery chin going nineteen to the dozen. If she caught a group of us chatting in a corridor, she would swoop down with amazing speed to suggest we go over to the church next door and have a chat to Our Lord or even to Father in the confessional if we want to get something off our chests.

"Yes, sister", we'd say before sloping off to a place that Sister Mary couldn't get to, like the boiler room in the basement where our P.E. kits were kept and which was only accessible by a flight of steep steps.

Sister Mary climbed up into our Portakabin classroom and began her usual patrol around the desks.

"Disgraceful," she said grabbing a handful of Patricia's hair. Having obviously forgotten the rule about long hair being tied up, Patricia blushed as Sister Mary told her off in a voice that weaved in and out like an accordion. Sister Mary held on to Patricia's locks as she spoke. Perhaps she had forgotten what hair felt like, or remembered her own at Patricia's age before her vocation required the sacrificing of it to a pair of sharp scissors.

"Only street gerrulls paint their nails," she scolded, having moved on to my friend, Simone. Again, perhaps it was the contact with another human being that made her hold Simone's hand like a dainty glove during the scolding.

It was hard to sit up straight for very long on the stools provided and Winnie had begun to collapse down into herself.

"No slouching!" said Sister Mary, sticking a bony knee in Winnie's back. I daren't look at Win and reverted instead to gazing out of the window. I thanked my lucky stars that I wasn't guilty of any misdemeanours myself. Having recently starred in *The Lady of Shalott* a re-enactment of Tennyson's poem directed by Mrs Walter, I thought myself above reproach. I was lulled into a sense of false security however as Sister Mary's face, birdy and bespectacled suddenly loomed up in front of my own.

"And no stargazin'!" she yelled as I jumped out of my skin. It never paid to relax around Sister Mary. She then went on to lecture us about not wearing our hats in church and how we should always remember that we represented the school wherever we were. Luckily, she hadn't witnessed some of the girls hanging around the town after hours with their ties undone and their hats over their eyes like gangsters.

Sister Mary's parting shot before leaving Sister Pius to get on with the lesson was a reminder about what it would take to get into heaven and live in paradise for all eternity.

"Just think of that when you are tempted into sin," she said. "Eternity, eternity, eternity..."

Her duty done for the day, Sister Mary clambered back out onto the path and took off across the garden like a giant magpie, her veil flying out behind her.

A few months later when the school closed due to lack of funds. Some of us who passed our Eleven-Plus were sent to the grammar school for a late entrance exam. Those who hadn't been busy stargazing were accepted, so it was secondary school for me, the Lady of Shalott herself.

A few years after the nuns returned to Ireland, I heard of the passing of Sister Mary and a rumour that Sister Pius had left the Order.

As for Win and I, our dance lessons didn't last very long once we started going to the local discos and clubs. We found a pair of gorgeous satin dresses on the Saturday market for our debut. They were A-line style, covered in a sort of crochet work of the same colour. Win's was red and mine blue. We were fourteen and very grown up or so we thought. We could even order a fruit juice in a pub for goodness sake! However, this was soon swapped for Babycham and Mrs Ridley's dedicated tuition replaced by head banging to Jeff Beck with our hair over our faces.

Schoolchums

29

Square

Our house was one of several around what we called 'the square'. Having only three sides it was really a large cul-de-sac with a stretch of green beyond it known as 'the triangle'. Here, tradesmen pitched up: the fruit and veg lorry, the baker's truck, the milk float and various ice-cream wagons. The dustcart arrived once a week with its chimp mascot tied on the front and the men scuffing along the paths with bins on their shoulders. The old skirted lamp post that once stood outside our house was great for climbing on or swinging out from at the end of a rope, despite warnings from my mother, often at the end of her own – rope, I mean – that we would fall off and break our necks. She needn't have worried as it wasn't long before Ashford Council saw fit to replace the lamp post with a smooth, totally un-climbable version.

In winter of course the square took on a different aspect. There were few cars on the roads back then and the snow was never cleared but just lay where it fell until it melted. The street would be eerily silent after a snow fall and the only sounds were the cries of us kids making snowmen or joining the queue for the long slide in the middle of the road.

My father could often be found shaving in the kitchen mirror of an evening. The steaminess of the place would blur his reflection and he would often go out with a couple of bloody scraps of paper adorning his chin. When I got older I would share the mirror space with him, making up my face like 'Painted Polly' as he called me. The scene would be reminiscent of the one from the W.C. Fields' film *It's A Gift* in which the unfortunate Mr Bissonette competes with his daughter for the bathroom mirror.

My father's finishing touch to his toilette was to push a steel comb through his hair, which unlike Mr Bissonette's was thick and dark and known to myself and my siblings as 'The Petrified Forest'. If he knew were watching, Father would then give a brief tug to each side of his scalp as though fitting on a cap for comedy effect.

"Whassup?" he would ask in his Irish brogue as we sniggered. His shaving equipment was kept in the over-sink cupboard and more often than not, Father would leave the topping up of his blade supply until the last minute, so that one of us would be despatched to the barber's at the end of the street for some '7 O'Clocks'. I remember the wallpaper in the barber's hallway being a fascinating blend of cartoons and newspaper cuttings, real 60s stuff, but there was never much time to stand admiring it as my father would be would be waiting impatiently with a face full of shaving foam.

The jungle of nettles and bindweed that was our back garden when we first arrived in Twelve Acres was soon replaced by a trellis of honeysuckle and roses – all my mother's doing. Father's contribution was the planting of a small tree in the middle of the lawn and the installation of a swing made from metal piping which he embedded in concrete. Both lasted the duration of our childhoods and beyond.

On a summer's evening in 1966 my two sisters stood waiting patiently on the garden path. They were my 'bridesmaids' in a play I'd made up about a wedding, (my own) and were dressed in remnants of material with flowers in their hair. Both had been bribed with being allowed to stay up until our mother returned from work in exchange for taking part.

After groping around in the kitchen cupboard, I found what I'd been looking for – a long piece of net curtaining buried beneath a pile of mother's knitting patterns which I needed for my 'veil'. As I retrieved the netting, a young Roger Moore floated to the lino – Ivanhoe and Simone Templar in a yellow cardy.

Stuffing Roger back into the cupboard, I hurried out to the garden where I fastened the netting to my head before getting into position with the two girls behind me. My veil was slightly wonky due to their differing heights – one being eight and the other four – but we made the best of it. My imaginary bridegroom was 'Adam Adamant', played by Gerald Harper in the TV series about a handsome Victorian hero who got frozen in ice, only to be found on a building site a hundred years later. After being revived in hospital, Adam checked himself out and embarked on a series of weekly adventures screened on Saturday evenings. In his elegant cloak and waistcoat, swordstick at his side, imaginary Adam accompanied me up the garden path. In my hand I clutched a bunch of honeysuckle with a red rose in the middle – one of several planted by mother beside the lawn. 'Ena Harkness' read the label on its stem. The rose was the most perfect shape and its colour the deepest damask. When I buried my nose in it I was transported momentarily to another world, that of Ena, who I imagined rich and beautiful with a garden full of such roses all grown by hand.

Meanwhile, another Ena could be heard through next door's window. This was Ena Sharples of *Coronation Street*.

As we began our promenade along the garden path towards the back door, two faces appeared from behind the shed. They were sophisticated friends from convent school, Simone and Pam. Both wore make-up and the latest psychedelic patterned dresses. Both looked at me for an explanation.

I quickly ripped the veil from my head and shoo-ed my sisters away as though the 'wedding' had been all their idea. Bloomin' kids!

Simone and I had been friends since we were little. Both our fathers worked in the local railway factory and hailed from Cork. Simone smiled in sympathy as though despite her only-child status, she understood what it was like to have siblings who rope you into silly games (if this had been the case, which of course it hadn't). Pam however was clearly not convinced and looked at me sidelong. She'd had her doubts about me ever since I played the princess and kissed Patricia on the lips, even though I didn't enjoy it one bit. She never really understood acting or theatre, or anything much other than hanging around looking for boys, that was the trouble with Pam as far as I was concerned.

Sitting at the kitchen table with tumblers of orange squash, we discussed the Monkees. I was just about to chime in that *I'm A Believer* was my favourite song when Pam asked which one I'd like to sleep with.

"Davy Jones," I said in a low voice, in should this piece of information be overheard by the neighbour taking in her washing before part two of *Corrie*.

Taking an Embassy from her handbag Simone went to the gas stove to light it. I tried not to think of my father arriving back early from work to find handbags littering our table and Simone holding her hair up while lighting a fag from the gas. He couldn't stand smoking and wasn't keen on my friends hanging around the place, so it would've been a double whammy for sure.

"You ought to come up town one Friday night," suggested Simone as if this is the way to form a liaison with the preferred Monkee.

"OK," I said confidently.

On the Friday designated for my meeting with Simone, I stood admiring myself at the dressing table mirror. I had rolled my school skirt up a few inches and pulled some of my hair into an elastic band. The look I was aiming for was 'Sharon' on *Please Sir*, one of several TV role models back then. I hadn't quite mastered it though, despite lots of pouting in the mirror and spit-and-rub on mascara.

My mother was watching *Take Your Pick* with her Friday night bag of toffees tucked down the side of the chair. In our house, if anyone had sweets and wanted to hold onto them, it was best to keep them hidden.

When I asked for thruppence for a bag of chips (back then in pre-decimalisation 1966, thruppence meant three large old pennies or a three-penny bit, a twelve sided coin with the Queen's head on one side and a portcullis on the other) my mother delved into her handbag which occupied the space between the armchair and the hearth. It wasn't her best handbag, the black patent one that accompanied her to dances with my father at the Labour club down the road or St Simon's church hall in South Ashford, but an upright affair in red leather with two handles and zip in the middle. Access to this bag by anyone other than my mother was forbidden. God knows why when all it contained was a small diary, a handkerchief, some Nulon hand cream, a couple of photos of us older kids taken when we were small in Victoria Park and a clip-topped purse. From the latter that she took out a thruppenny bit and handed it to me.

"Don't be late in," she warned.

"No," I said at the same time as the contestant during the 'Yes and No Interlude' on *Take Your Pick*. As he was gonged out by Michael Miles' assistant, Bob Danvers-Walker, the audience erupted. I chose the moment to slip out, avoiding further questioning regarding the length of my skirt and amount of mascara on my eyes.

Simone was on the wall by the alley. Pam wasn't with her – a mercy. My school skirt would only have fuelled her suspicions that as well as being a bit strange, I had nil fashion sense. Simone took out her brush and began working on my hair. We didn't go to the chip shop straight away, which was a bit of a blow as I was always in the mood for a thruppenny bag with cracklings, but up the nearby alley and along Mill View. Simone said she knew some boys who lived in nearby Osborne Road so we might as well walk down there.

There were a couple of boys kicking a ball around outside the post office. Simone asked if they'd seen the ones she knew, but they hadn't. Meanwhile, I just loitered on the pavement looking up and down the road expectantly.

We eventually got our chips and hung around outside the shop for a bit. Simone soon got bored with the boys that congregated there, shouting and burping and wheeling about on their bikes. She called them square and juvenile. When she got on the bus for town I had the feeling she thought I was square too as she blew smoke out of the top deck window. I made my way up Twelve Acres, a failed dancer, actor and now a less than interesting companion. It was nearly dark and a game of rounders was going on in the square. The 'Sharon' look was replaced by my usual tomboy garb when I ran indoors, yanked on my stretchy trousers and rushed out to join the game. Growing up might have to wait a bit longer.

Back then, on those summer evenings, there was a sweetness in the air all mixed up with chip shop and railway dust and grass and something else – probably being young with all my life ahead of me – yes, I think it was something like that.

I occasionally talk about those old days to my young nieces as they sit hunched over Facebook. Being now classed as young adults they aren't interested in my reminiscences from the dark old times before they were born. Nevertheless, they do their best to indulge their auntie, who I think they see as being slightly 'ment-awl' with a nod and a smile as I prattle on about milk tokens, chilblains, 'Knock Down Ginger' and Ovaltine.

Once, when I gave a couple of them a lift to town where they were going clubbing, I asked if they wouldn't be cold without their coats. They just laughed and headed off like a bunch of wild ponies. Of course I had forgotten how hot gets in nightclubs and how uncool it is to be seen carrying your coat over your arm, even in the middle of winter. Was it really that long ago since I went from club to club, oblivious to the cold, borne up on a wave of Babycham-induced euphoria?

Obviously now regarded as some sort of mascot, I gathered my woolly cardigan tighter around me, turned up the heater and drove off feeling a bit like that old chimp on the front of the dustcart all those years ago.

Roger Moore in cardy

I WANNA BE FREE...

Davy Jones 1945 – 2012

My father, me and 'bridesmaids'
Anne and Cath

The Square – winter 1965
(I think I'm the one with the legs)

The Square now

School Daze

The move to my new school came as a nasty shock. I had thought myself quite brave and outgoing after my successes at the convent, but now I was one of a large crowd. There wasn't much in the way of drama on the curriculum at all as I remember.

An old battleaxe called Miss Brake took history. All tweed suit and hairnet, she was a bit like Margaret Rutherford, minus the joviality. She kept banging on about Albert Schweitzer and when she doled out loads of homework on him in those pre-Internet days I didn't know where to start.

The French teacher was English but did his best to look Gallic all the time by wearing a beret. When he pronounced the word 'tu' he'd make his mouth into a complete circle and encouraged us to do the same. It was embarrassing if he made you do it on your own in class when reading out loud about the Marceau family and their dog Bruno.

"Repetez! Tu!...Tu!" he'd insist if you tried a slack lipped 'Too'. 'Vous' was easier, although a girl who clearly hadn't been paying attention once pronounced it 'Vows' causing teacher's eyes to widen and a gasp to ripple through the classroom.

The music teacher was just plain mad. If I wasn't talking of the past I would say he resembled the doc in the film *Back to the Future*.

"Oooo! Listen to the Tee Dium!" he'd yell in a voice uncannily like that of Frankie Howerd – *("Oooo, listen to Francis!")*.

From Latin with Sister Pius, I reckoned the pronunciation should probably have been 'Tay Dayum', but 'Frankie' probably had his own reasons for using "Tee Dium" – the lack of enthusiasm from the class for a start, (myself included).

The blue boxes that he handed out contained metal keys which had long since lost their tune. Plonk away as I might, I could never distinguish one note from another.

My musical taste was Radio One but on the transistor radio I got free with so many cereal packet tops I managed to tune in to Johnnie Walker's programme on Radio Caroline one night. After that, I twiddled with the dial so much in an attempt to find the pirate ship again, that the lettering wore off. I blamed this for the disappearance of Johnnie Walker until a classmate enlightened me – the ship was no longer broadcasting. Didn't I watch the news? No, not really. I never went in for current affairs, preferring to live in a sort of dazed fantasy world of my own. This would definitely come back on me in the future.

I loathed gym. I could never quite grasp what we were supposed to be doing for a start. Why couldn't we have dancing instead? I'd spend each lesson climbing up and down the wall ladder like a deranged beetle. When the games mistress insisted I attempt to jump the horse one afternoon, I duly queued up. Leap-frogging over a partner wasn't too bad – at least the human body has some give in it – but that horse thing seemed to be built along the same dimensions as the one the Greeks used to enter the gates of Troy. I ran up to it with an air of excited anticipation burning in my eyes, only to bottle out at the last minute due to a sudden spasm in my knee joint. I hopped away clutching the affected area with a grimace of pain on my face.

Over the following weeks it was the left knee, then the right knee, an ankle, a sudden stomach ache. When I'd exhausted my arsenal of excuses, I would be off sick or in desperation, revert to beetling up and down the ladder until the teacher wasn't looking. I would then slip out to the toilets for the remainder of the lesson. Judo was almost bearable as Emma Peel in *The Avengers* was another role model of mine, but even then there was a lot of standing about between throws so that this too bordered on the tedious.

Netball was far too violent – a lot of yelling and pushing and leaping while passing the ball back and forth (I never quite got it even though the rules were explained to me over and over.) Like hockey, which we touched on at the convent school it was so boring that my brain just wouldn't take it in. I only knew rounders and threw myself into that but was thwarted when the hard little ball hit me in the eye. A tennis ball was used for the games in the square at home where it would get slogged as far as the houses opposite or half way down the road to get in the maximum number of rounds. Surely, that was the purpose of the game so why the useless ball?

The needlework class was interminable with the teacher's favourites gathered about her desk all afternoon as she demonstrated stitching techniques. I remember attempting to make a nightdress in stiff, bright red cotton with white stars on.

"Whatever's that?" she asked one day when I'd plucked up the courage to ask her a question.

"A nightie," I offered.

She pointed out that the material was totally unsuitable for 'a nightie' and good luck with sleeping in it. (I missed Sister Pius!)

However, if I think I had it 'tough' (this brings to mind that famous Monty Python sketch where the three old guys are sitting round a table comparing who had the worst upbringing – *"We used to have to lick road clean wi' tongue..."*) these schooldays were joyous compared to those of a friend of mine. Dipi was brought up in Tanzania and one day in school had turned to tell the kid behind to stop tapping her. The teacher saw only Dipi talking in class. Her punishment consisted of a hard pinch of the skin underneath the top of her arm, followed by several strokes of the ruler on the knuckles through which a pencil was threaded for maximum effect. After this she was made to circle the classroom on her knees. She was eight years old at the time.

Cookery, otherwise known as 'domestic science', wasn't much fun either. The only science to it was that of trying to prepare something edible while sharing the mixing bowls and oven space with everyone else. My raspberry buns looked like flattened bosoms, a circle of hardened sponge with a tiny nipple of jam in the middle, hardly Elizabeth David.

My stuffed eggs weren't too bad until they met with a slight accident on the way home. As I turned right into Hunter Avenue from Hythe Road, the tin containing these delicious morsels slipped from my handlebars to the ground and rolled across to the forecourt of the Fox pub. Stuffed eggs to mayonnaise mix in one simple manoeuvre – oh well.

In 1969 Neil Armstrong walked on the moon, Butch and Sundance were released onto the big screen and Maggie Smith won the BAFTA for the title role in *The Prime of Miss Jean Brodie*. Like Jean, my maths teacher was slim and hailed from Scotland, but there the similarity ended. While fictional Jean referred to her pupils as the 'crème de la crème', sharing her romantic view of the world with them, the all too real 'Highland Terror' would bark on about fractions, logs and decimals, chalking them on the board with a passion.

As the numbers flew up with a point here and a slash there and "och, isn't it all so easy?" I tried to keep a low profile from the back of the room. My main problem was of course that I didn't bloody well get it. I really didn't have a clue.

I thought I was in luck one morning when my desk mate offered me her book to crib from. All was well until the Terror asked me to demonstrate how I'd arrived at my conclusion. That day my nails were covered in violet coloured polish. (Sister Mary would have had a fit, God rest her). The Terror likened these to my mathematical ability – shabby. I removed the polish when I got home, wishing I could remove either the Terror or preferably myself from the school so easily.

My form teacher, Mr Monk also happened to be the English master and provided the only respite in an otherwise depressing couple of years. His lessons were always interesting, despite his air of having long since despaired of getting through to us about anything much, let alone the classics. Mr Monk, with his great stories and love of language read Shakespeare with the delivery of a stage actor. He'd play Shylock to our Portias in *The Merchant of Venice* and Romeo to our Juliets. Having been picked out one afternoon to read Julius Caesar to his Brutus, I put my speech training from the convent school into practice and I did the best I could 'with feeling'. Mr Monk seemed quite impressed.

"Come back and see us," he said jovially the day we filed out of his class for the last time. He obviously meant in a year or two or preferably never, but believing that a special link had been forged between us and that he'd be nothing short of delighted, I took him up on the invitation a few months later, catching him before his afternoon class.

"Can I help you?" he asked with a puzzled expression.

'Et tu, Brute,' I thought to myself as I sloped away dejectedly.

Dreamland was the amusement park in Margate that as a child I used to adore visiting. But at the age of fifteen, it was a different story. To be spotted by your pals there with your family wasn't only unfashionable it was actually quite terrifying. One Sunday my father insisted I tag along. For some reason he didn't trust me not to let friends into the house and wreak havoc if left home alone. To see him with the kids on the scenic railway bellowing with laughter was just too embarrassing. Why couldn't he be a cool kind of dad, all hair and glasses like Manfred Mann?

The only attraction I wanted to visit was the fortune teller, but Father said it was a waste of time and money and who wanted to know the future anyway? Stuck back there in 1968 with not a lot going for me – I did.

"There must be some kinda way outta here..." sang Hendrix over the whine of the bumper cars. Yes, there must. Where the hell was it?

My two kid sisters were enjoying the ride with me at the wheel, but I kept my head down, making steering rather difficult so that we got bumped to within an inch of our lives.

I managed to keep a low profile and all was well until we got to the cafeteria. It was too late for *Quadrophenia,* but teenagers still moved in packs. When I sighted a bunch of my friends breezing past, I turned away quickly, but not before Tracey, a girl with whom I was in competition over the same boy spotted me. When she called my name I had no choice but to turn and feign surprise at seeing her. Tracey always had the right gear on and that Sunday was no exception – mauve leather jacket, short, neatly styled hair, a tiny clutch bag under her arm. Batting her eyelashes in astonishment at seeing me there with my entourage, she resembled Bette Davis in some classy old movie while I felt like Mary Poppins.

The kids were having a great time. As they squeezed ketchup on their chips from a large plastic tomato, I rolled my eyes if to confirm to Tracey that I was there under duress. She pointed me out to the group standing near the rifle range, one of which was the boy previously referred to. On seeing me he grinned at Tracey and proceeded to pepper a metal strip with pellets. There was no competition of course – who was I kidding? I took my place at the cafe table with my ego similarly peppered.

Ian, my future husband, eight years my junior, used to be taken on holiday with his parents to Margate. For all I know I could have passed him that day, a young lad chomping on a toffee apple, riding on the bumper cars, emerging from a sack at the bottom of the helter skelter, or running out of the Ghost Train (there were more scares to come did he but know it).

Years later, our wedding also had the air of amusement park as it took place in Las Vegas. While people screamed on the roller coaster ride nearby, Ian and I tied the knot at the Graceland Wedding Chapel, the venue for such famous weddings as that of Jon and Dorothea Bon Jovi and the Thomson Twins.

The handsome Elvis I ordered was unable to make it and I nearly flipped when a five foot nothing Mexican man appeared in a bright green outfit complete with cape. Mercifully, he was there for his own wedding which followed our own. The replacement Elvis was an older version with a built up shoe. He turned out to be terrific once he got going. The only trouble was that instead of just of a verse or two of *I Can't Help Falling In Love* he insisted on doing the whole song, leaving the pair of us with nothing to do but stare at each other for ages (embarrassment factor – high).

Other song choices were *Treat Me Like a Fool* which Nicholas Cage sings to Laura Dern in the David Lynch film *Wild At Heart* and *The Wonder of You* in which those assembled joined in with gusto.

As we made our way to our reception past the roller coaster rides, I remembered my late father laughing on the scenic railway back in Margate all those years ago and wished he was there. He was right about the fortune teller of course. It's a good thing we can't see into the future.

Our Wedding, Las Vegas 2006

The Day Job

My first job was at the Kent Paper Company in South Willesborough. My salary was £6 a week and my duties were copy-typing, covering the switchboard and sending out the post.

I'd been studying shorthand and typing since I was thirteen at Miss Butcher's establishment off the Hythe Road, my father being determined that I should have a skill which would supply me with an income

Years of key-bashing, scribbling and phone-answering later, I would realise how sensible it was to have these skills to fall back on. The trouble is that having fallen back on them I never quite get up again, but at the age of sixteen, I was blissfully unaware of this.

Occasionally, if his secretary was away, I would be called in to the manager's office to take dictation. I was always extremely nervous; despite Miss Butcher's tuition I could never read back what I had taken down. The Pitman outlines were replaced by what looked like Egyptian hieroglyphs. (code-breaker, Alan Turing would have had his work cut out with me during the war.) When I managed to type a supplier's order for thirty rolls of paper instead of three the manager scrawled across the page in horror.

South Willesborough was a sleepy old place back then in the summer of '69, uncluttered with cars and a river running through it – not a river as large as the Blackfoot in Montana which features in the film *A River Runs Through It* starring Robert Redford, but the quietly trickling Stour.

I would stroll home through the fields and across the railway bridge at lunch time. Glen Campbell's *Wichita Lineman* being in the charts then will always bring to mind the smell of coal dust and the track shimmering away to infinity.

It seemed like it was all happening over there in America. What with Butch and Sundance about to become famous for their on screen leaping and shooting, and Glen needing and wanting for all time, I wondered whether my life was going to consist of walking over that bridge every day to type invoices. Clackity-clack ping! Where was my glamorous acting career?

"Stargazin'…" whispered Sister Mary, or was it the breeze ruffling through the grass?

Simone came to work in the front office with me as a temp. We drove Mr Barron, the office manager half mad with our silly behaviour. If Simone was around when I used the tannoy to summon factory personnel to the phone, I could barely get the words out for sniggering – so much for the English Speaking Exam.

On returning from lunch one day, I found Simone listening wide-eyed as filing clerk Edie, an old fashioned girl described her lunchtime snack of Kettle Bender – bread and cheese with hot water poured over it. Simone and I fell about laughing like the little spacemen in the Cadbury's Smash advert.

"A little less noise please," cautioned Mr Barron when our hysterics had caused the Manager to complain from his sanctum down the corridor. He already had reservations about me since that potential bulk order which would probably have folded the business had it been shipped. What would he have done with all that paper? Mummified me while I was still alive probably. Oh, well, at least I would have been biodegradable.

It was all very well giggling over Edie's soggy cheese sandwich, but as a kid I ate bread and milk with sugar on to keep out the winter's chill, and my mother often referred to having eaten Cocoa Sop – bread dipped in cocoa when she was small. (I blame the war).

When I'd finish a pile of invoices I would take them to the accounts department along the corridor, where two lovely old dames, Agnes and Maude sat puffing away on cigarettes. Agnes would often be entering cheques into an ancient-looking ledger, while Maude tapped the calculator, or adding machine as it was known then, with a pen, her gnarled old fingers heavy with rings. Bertie, a gangly lad with a mushroom hairstyle, smoked as much as Agnes and Maude, so that mid-afternoon, they were all sitting in a regular pea-souper. This den of iniquity was overseen – as much as it was possible to see anything in there – by the aforementioned Mr Barron. I'd grope my way in with the invoices and put them down somewhere to be found once the fog had cleared.

The squeak of the tea trolley would announce the arrival of Nellie, a gentle soul with the face of a comfy old cat. Simone and I would loiter about the trolley, taking ages to make up our minds between a Mars, a Kit-Kat or a Ripple.

Another ruse to spend time doing something other than typing invoices was an extended trip to the loo for the re-touching of make-up (in case I hadn't got enough on already) and an examination of my general appearance in the full length mirror. I was sixteen going on seventeen, but Leisl from *The Sound of Music* I wasn't. Teenage fashions were awful in '69 and if you came from neighbourhood you were either a skinhead (short hair and skirts to match if you hung around with bovver boys and lunatics) or a 'grebo' (long hair, long skirt if you hung around with bikers and hippies). Like most of my friends I hung out with the skinheads, so my hair was cropped on top with straggly sides and a short spiky fringe. A less flattering hairstyle would have been hard to find, but back then in the murky sludge of teenage, I felt I had to look like everyone else. Add to this my monkey jumper, short skirt and big clumpy shoes, and you had Florence from *The Magic Roundabout* meets *The Bride of Frankenstein* (I was born in a thunderstorm after all).

My admiring of myself was interrupted one day by the arrival of Maude, who proceeded to take a bottle of turquoise coloured liquid from her handbag and swig it. Countless years spent tapping the adding machine were clearly having an effect. With dear Maude in mind I resolved to make some serious changes to my life. Firstly, I would change my job, and secondly my wardrobe. Despite already being high on the fashion police's list of offenders, I invested in a double-breasted mac in antique leather (that's plastic, let's face it), which had a wide belt and an even wider buckle. On my feet I sported a pair of flat brown chiselled-toed shoes with buckles on each. Standing in the bus queue outside Pricerite's in the high street one evening, I spotted a female dressed as an film extra from *Cromwell* reflected in the window. I begin to snigger until I realised it was me.

'Florence' with baby brother 1970

Ashford High Street 1965. A lorry obscures the 'Cromwellian'
lurking outside Pricerites.
(Copyright The Francis Frith Collection)

The Hopeless Hippy

In London I shared a flat on the ground floor of a dingy house near the Oval cricket ground. It wasn't my flat of course – young people didn't buy flats back then in 1971. Taking on a mortgage was something you envisaged doing in the far distant future when you had settled down with Mr Right or even Mr Wrong. Until then, if you had any sense, you were out having fun. My rent of £3.50 entitled me to half a bedroom plus the use of the kitchen and dining room. There was an outside toilet and no bathroom. The bath was in the kitchen, next to the stove, covered by a board when not in use. Domestic health and safety didn't apply quite so much back then. People had lived in those houses during the blitz when the prospect of getting spattered by a frying sausage while bathing didn't hold quite the same degree of threat.

I shared the bedroom with Bronwen, a downbeat girl from Cardiff who hid behind long hair and whose answer to everything was "I should doubt it, love."

Kitty, who had the main bedroom was a 'right on' sort of person and extremely kind. I never quite understood why she didn't get custody of her three pale little girls who would visit for the weekend now and then. (Their father would often call the visit off at the last minute and Kitty would retire devastated to her room). Kitty lectured at a local college and attended Angela Davis meetings in Brixton, campaigning for black people's rights. She seemed preoccupied with the rights of others when her own were sadly neglected.

Kitty's boyfriend Julian, an ex-junkie, would turn up at all hours, often in a state. In the mornings after we all left for work he'd remain in Kitty's room trying to get his head together. He and Kitty went off to Paris one weekend but the trip wasn't a great success. Someone went up and punched Julian while he and Kitty picnicked on the banks of the Seine – God knows why, unless his attacker was incited to violence by people with vacant expressions.

Kitty related this event while cooking fish fingers as I soaked in the bath. The unprovoked assault was just another example of the bad luck that seemed to dog both their lives.

As Kitty's life was hard and full of horrible happenings, so Bronwen's was safe and uneventful. She had a mundane job in the City and her weekends consisted of food shopping at Safeway's in Stockwell and knitting in the dining room to the music of Emerson Lake and Palmer. She always had money, hoarded it like squirrel, whereas my wages were all gone by Sunday night – blown on enjoying myself.

We had a party in the flat once and Bronwen burst unexpectedly into life over Robert Parker's *Barefootin'*. By the next morning though, she had reverted to her usual mousy self, only with a headache.

Having made the transition from skinhead to hippy, I was often found playing the likes of T.Rex, Led Zeppelin and Free on my Dansette record player. I started hanging around with some 'hairy' friends of Kitty's and we'd head off to live music bars, such as the Greyhound in Fulham Palace Road. One December evening we went up to Alexandra Palace to see 'Zep'. The one pound entry fee made a dent in my weekend budget and we had to walk a lot of the way home, but hey, what the hell – it was rock and roll, right? (It was also very cold).

I returned to the flat one Monday evening to find Kitty teary-eyed and smoking a joint. As often happened, the ex had messed her around over access to the kids that weekend.

"Can I have some of that?" I asked. It seemed a natural request for a hippy to make after all.

"Have you smoked it before?" asked Kitty, conscious of my own well being despite her own trauma.

"Oh, yes, of course!" I assured her. "Loads of times!"

I hadn't though.

"Never has any effect on me," I said after a few drags. "I knew it wouldn't."

I suddenly began to feel ever so slightly and then very definitely sick. I'd had faggots for dinner and wasn't really sure what these consist of, but suspected I was about to find out.

Oscar Wilde said *"I might be lying in the gutter, but some of us are gazing at the stars"*. In my case, it was the floor of the outside loo that I was lying on while gazing at the night sky. Convinced that my life was about to end I thought for a moment that I saw Sister Mary out of the corner of my eye, her dark skirts swishing. I was clearly going to join her in eternity far sooner than I'd envisaged and she'd arrived at the toilet door to collect me, the fallen stargazer. As it happened I was given a reprieve and it was in fact Bronwen in her maxi coat who obscured my view of the solar system.

"I don't think smoking suits her, do you?" asked Kitty.

"I should doubt it, love," came the reply.

Soon afterwards, Bronwen met an Aussie postman and set off to a new life 'down under'. I moved to a flat in Ealing where I made some life-long friends. The place was on several floors above a dry cleaners and so seedy out the back that it was often a prime location for film shoots like *The Sweeney*. In one episode some gangsters were seen leaping over our back wall onto the dustbins.

Along the road in Shepherds Bush lived lovely Auntie Rose, who resembled the actress Kathleen Harrison, star of the 60s sitcom, *Mrs Thursday*. My father had taken me to visit Rose, (who was married to his uncle Bob) when I was a child, so I got in touch and we stayed good friends from then on. Rose's maisonette in Adelaide Grove hadn't changed very much since the old days. Access to the back garden was gained via steps from a trap door in the kitchen floor. In later years, Rose opted for the easier approach to hanging out her washing – reeling it back and forth through the window over the sink.

Rose's front room wallpaper consisted of huge green leaves so that you felt you were sitting in Kew Gardens or a giant marijuana plantation (bearing mind my experience with this, I prefer Kew). In the corner was a bar with a pair of maracas and a straw donkey brought back from various holidays in Spain. Once, when my sisters were staying with me in the 'Sweeney' flat we managed to lock ourselves out and arrived at Rose's front door to find a party in full swing. Rose was wearing a paper doily on her head and upstairs guests were twirling about to *Y Viva España*. Typically, Rose gave us all her bed and slept the night on the sofa.

Rose had met Bob when she was working at Heinz and he was a scene shifter for the BBC. I was jealous as a kid to learn that their daughter, my cousin Maureen had featured as an extra in a film when she was a few months old. Rose had a heart of gold and any relatives and friends passing through London were always made welcome.

Rose disliked Christmas since Bob's death and would often reminisce about those gone by. I last saw her in Hammersmith Hospital where, in her late eighties, she had been admitted with pneumonia. It was Christmas Eve and she whispered that she felt she was going to be moved the next day, and so she was.

I had set out for her funeral one morning in early January but due to frozen points the train I was on ground to a standstill for hours and I missed the service at Mortlake Crematorium. The power went down while I was in the toilet and the door wouldn't budge. I was eventually freed after about twenty minutes and emerged into the corridor where a small crowd had gathered out of curiosity. Auntie Rose would have laughed – bless.

Working in a fashion house you'd think I might've picked up some tips on clothes. However, this proved not to be the case. Employed as a secretary-model as opposed to a model secretary (which at that stage I certainly was not), I often had to abandon the typewriter and put on various garments for potential buyers. Having progressed from skinhead to hippy via a brush with Cromwell, I often turned out for work in a pair of brown flared trousers and a corduroy smock top in yellow with green sleeves. My hair, a wild mass of untamed frizz was left to do its own thing.

Helen, the designer seemed less than impressed by my attire for some reason.

"Whatever are you wearing?" she asked on the eve of an important customer's visit. "You'd better choose something from the range to wear tomorrow – the old end I mean, not anything from the latest designs."

The range consisted mainly of evening wear as far as I could see, apart from puffed-sleeved blouse in broderie anglaise and a long dress in the style of a butcher's apron.

I may have put my aspirations of becoming an actress on hold for the time being, but on catching sight of myself in a shop window the following morning, I could've be about to audition for *The Good Old Days*. The only thing missing to top off the whole dubious outfit might have been a straw boater. Whether Helen's design for the skirt was to blame or a slip of the cutter's scissors, I don't know, but for some reason the skirt kept wrapping itself around my legs as I made my way to the tube station.

"For your delectation..." I heard Leonard Sachs announce from his box at the side of the stage, "An extraordinary vision of timeless sartorial elegance..."

"Oooo!" went the audience appreciatively.

"Bloody hell!" said I in an attempt to keep on a pair of slippery sandals. Like the rest of the get-up, it was their first day out. The soles were bound to my feet by four bits of string which kept working lose no matter how tight I tied them. They looked OK in the flea market, but put to the test in the street they failed miserably. I arrived at work with aching calf muscles and my toes sore from clinging on for dear life. The important client came in and was impressed enough to order a couple of the outfits that I modelled. Not surprisingly, the butcher's apron was not among them.

Reuben, the proprietor of the fashion house had a strange affliction in that he couldn't stop touching things. For example, if he put something down on a table he couldn't just leave it, but had to keep touching the object, then the his nose, then the table or the object again and then his nose. I noticed he did it all the more when he got confused or over-excited.

"Reuben, stop it!" warned his mother, Miriam, when she'd catch him at it.

"Stop what?" Reuben would reply, touching and sniffing.

On one occasion he was unable to let go of the pen he was trying to put down and kept tapping the surface of the desk with it until Miriam was obliged to physically prize the thing from his hand. His problem prevented him from making deliveries and more often than not he would arrive back with the item of clothing he had meant to leave behind. For that reason I was sent on errands to various boutiques and warehouses with armfuls of Helen's samples. Having fallen in love with David Bowie and added *Ziggy Stardust and the Spiders From Mars* album to my record collection, I was amazed when on visiting a firm near Piccadilly I found myself standing in the same spot as divine David on the cover! His space boots and my shoes had trod the same bit of pavement it seemed! The phone box used for the back of the album was just around the corner! – Wow!

When I left the rag trade to be a junior secretary in a film distribution company, all traces of my bohemian lifestyle had to disappear. I had to be smart, punctual, and look vaguely efficient. On my first day, wearing my newly washed mac, I was pushing through the crowded Underground when a lady sidled up and touched my arm.

"Excuse me," she said.

"Yes?" I answered warily, thinking she might be a beggar or even a pickpocket, both of which would have been wasting their time with me.

"Do you know you've got a clothes peg on your hem?"

I glanced down to see the offending article which had sneakily accompanied me from home and whipped it off quickly. (Embarrassment factor – high.)

Pamela, the boss's secretary (the word personal assistant not in general use then), with her swooped up glasses and hair in a French roll, often hauled me over the coals. I forgot to read my work through properly, I lacked attention to detail, I was gauche (I told the boss not to come back 'sloshed' from a lunch meeting on learning that wine was to be served), and I was of course often late. If I returned from lunch a minute after two o'clock I would find an admonishing note on my typewriter. The shops in Oxford Street were usually the cause, or the stalls in nearby Berwick Street market.

I made a lot of tea and coffee for guests, ran errands and took down letters in my own brand of shorthand which Pamela called 'gobbledegook'. In the two years that I was under her wing I did everything from opening the post to polishing 'Young Winston', the rubber plant named after the film distributed by the company based on the life of Churchill.

An occasional bonus was being able to attend showings of new films. At a screening of *O Lucky Man*, director, Lindsay Anderson and some of his crew were attendance. Afterwards Mr Anderson asked us what we thought of the movie. A girl from accounts piped up that it reminded her of Stanley Kubrick's *A Clockwork*

Orange, probably because Malcolm McDowell appeared in both films. This clearly wasn't the answer Mr Anderson was looking for and he proceeded to 'collapse' into the arms of one of his colleagues. I always kept schtum during these sessions for fear of similarly putting my foot in it.

Two years whizzed by and it was time to move on. It was highly unlikely that Pamela would leave in the near future and even less likely that I'd be chosen to fill her shoes if she did. I joined a well known cinema advertising group whose offices overlooked Berwick Street market. My boss headed up a team of reps out on the road selling advertising to local tradesmen. They were a mixed bunch and often related amusing stories about the clients to my colleague Michelle and myself as we sat chortling.

When a group of actresses arrived one day to be filmed around the market for one of the company's productions, I couldn't help but feel envious. Wasn't I supposed to be doing something like that? What happened? To be an actress you needed training, a portfolio of photographs, an agent and good contacts, whereas I needed the 'proper job' just to survive. Nevertheless, on day two of the shoot and being a dedicated re-offender as far as fashion was concerned, I donned my most eye catching outfit, a bright yellow trouser suit in crimplene. I then proceeded to lurk around the market, putting myself in full view of the director. He was obviously not into his yellow period as I was asked to step back when, in a bid to literally break into the film business, I wandered into shot. I sloped off in disappointment. Perhaps if the commercial had been for Jaffa oranges I might've stood more of a chance.

I was therefore all the more devastated a few weeks later when Michelle was approached randomly on the street by another crew shooting an ad for chocolate. All she had to do was be herself, nibble a bit of choccie and hey presto – she was on TV a few weeks later looking fantastic!

As my services in front of the camera were clearly not required, I took on a temporary behind-the-scenes role as secretary to Mr Charles Schneer, producer of *Sinbad and the Eye of the Tiger*. In a chilly studio somewhere in Kensal Green, producer and special effects creator, Ray Harryhausen worked painstakingly, creating models and animating them for the movie.

Dotted around his workshop were models from his previous films including 'Kali', the six-armed goddess from *The Golden Voyage of Sinbad*, and the Centaur. Back there in the days before computer graphics, Mr Harryhausen used a technique called 'stop framing' which involved the laborious task of photographing every stage of the model character's movement before piecing the whole thing together on film.

It was a fun few weeks and at the end of my stay I was given a 'Sinbad' scarf as a memento.

At a theatrical agency based in Soho, I did more stargazing than ever. It was thrilling to meet famous actors and observe their success. There were also the upcoming ones who didn't always get the roles they were aiming for.

"Them's the breaks", my American boss would say.

While threading the message tapes through the telex machine in those days before the word processor or even the fax, I'd dream about becoming an actress, getting a big break in films and moving to Hollywood. The only 'break' I got was when the telex tape invariably snapped in half and I'd have to type the message all over again.

I often chatted on the phone to a girl called Diane who was working for a production company out at Shepperton Studios. They were making *The Land That Time Forgot* starring Doug McClure, known for his role as 'Trampas' in *The Virginian*. Diane's job sounded very exciting and she admitted that she had run into Doug once or twice.

"Lucky you!" I said.

(That same year Doug also starred in a TV film called *Satan's Triangle*, one of the most terrifying films I've ever seen. I managed to sit through this and *The Exorcist* safe in the belief that none of these things could really happen. As I got older I realised that they probably can and am now unable to watch anything remotely spooky).

When the filming came to an end several weeks later, Diane called to tell me she was leaving her job and going off to the States with none other than Doug himself! Bloody hell! It was like the end of Jane Eyre *('Reader, I married him!')* and so she did! She got Doug McClure and I got a Sinbad scarf.

Oh well – 'Them's the breaks'.

In the summer of 1980 I went into the theatre. Aside from being in the West End, it wasn't the one I'd been hoping for.

On a sunny afternoon in Willesborough when I was about eight years old, I'd set off for the post office in Osborne Road with a couple of pennies in my hand, one of which was very old and black, with Queen Victoria's head on. I used to like these old pennies and would hang onto them as long as possible until the desire for a Penny Arrow or a circle of liquorice with a pink sweet in the middle overcame all else. I was walking along Mill View when I suddenly felt quite removed from my body. I could see birds flapping about on the telegraph wires, hear the hum of the bees in the daisies by people's gates, see my shadow following diagonally behind me, but my mind wasn't there. It was as though I was watching myself walking along. The 'out of body' feeling continued until I reached the post office sweet counter and parted with the Victorian penny.

I was now having a similar experience on the Rosalind Chetwynd Ward at the Middlesex Hospital while trying to come to terms with some devastating news. Nurses were moving about, patients were talking to their visitors, but I was sitting on my bed feeling completely removed from everything going on around me. I could see my body, but felt that it belonged to someone else. At the time, I wished it did as I had just been told by an eminent surgeon, Stuart Steele, that I had a malignant tumour which was in danger of spreading. His planned course of action was six blasts of radiotherapy followed by a removal of the affected part – the womb. That meant no children of course, but there was a good chance of success if we got started as soon as possible.

I could hear all of this but I wasn't really taking it in. Up until then, I had been drifting along relatively happily in life, concerned with nothing other than my job and my boyfriend. Being told at twenty-five that I couldn't have a family was pretty devastating but when I began to get my head around it, this seemed a small price to pay for survival.

I had to find a way to break the news to my family. To many people back then, the word 'cancer' means sure and certain death, so I decided not to use it if I could avoid doing so, even to myself.

My father was an ex-heavyweight boxer and when I began to gather my wits, I decided to follow his example and go in fighting. The next day, he and my mother found me sitting on a bench in the garden of the Middlesex Hospital. I knew I had to be strong for their sake, and assured them that I was in the best hands.

I had tremendous support. My mother was always there at the other end of the phone, which would be wheeled over to my bed. My sister Mo would visit and chat. I did not feel alone.

The radium treatments were administered under general anaesthetic and during the days that followed them I was plagued with nausea.

On good days I'd be able to get down to the garden, but on others all I wanted to do was curl up on the bed. I always made an effort to appear positive, get dressed and put on make-up even if I felt lousy, partly for the benefit of my visitors and partly for my own. I might feel sick but I didn't have to look it. I refused to be bed-bound unless absolutely necessary and would often take a slow walk down to the garden or the little Byzantine chapel on the ground floor. (This lovely chapel still remains even though the hospital itself has been razed to the ground for a new development.) I could also go walkabout in the street if I was up to it, which made me feel remotely human, despite the weird things being done to me behind the hospital walls.

The nurses were around my own age and lightened things up with their jokes and general levity. They were always there with tea and chat in the early hours when I couldn't sleep. As they prepped me up for the first blast of radium, my life started to flash before me. I remembered with fondness my trips to the chip shop as a kid back in Twelve Acres. Now, I was 'frying tonight'. It wasn't the least bit funny of course, but I was young and time was on my side. Having complete faith in Mr Steele, it never really occurred to me that it might not be.

During my time at the Middlesex, the actor Peter Sellers was admitted to the private wing with a heart attack. When he died a few days later it was hard to believe that he who had played such brilliant characters as Inspector Clouseau ("*Is that your minkey?*") and Blue Bottle ("*You dirty, rotten swine!*") was no more.

While on the 'Roz Chet' I got to know several other patients, one of them a young Scottish girl called Janice who'd kind of lost her way. She'd got mixed up with a drug addict and had been living in a squat before being admitted to hospital with an ovarian problem. She dreaded being discharged because she had nowhere to go apart from an aunt in Scotland who was about to emigrate to the States. I asked why she didn't head up there, join her aunt and start a new life abroad, but the problem was money. The bus fare was fifteen pounds. Without much thought (as ever where money is concerned), I went to the bank, drew out the cash which I couldn't really afford and gave it to Janice.

My fellow patients told me I was mad and would never see the money again. It was bound to go on drugs – if not for Janice herself, then for her boyfriend. I left hospital for a few days' break prior to the operation itself and forgot all about everything including Janice, be she bussing up to Scotland or jacking up elsewhere, as I prepared myself for the big op.

The next stop for me was the Soho Hospital for Women. Later in life, on reading Andy Merriman's biography of Margaret Rutherford, *Dreadnought With Good*

Manners I discovered that in 1939 she acted in a charity performance of Oscar Wilde's *The Importance of Being Earnest* directed by John Gielgud in support of that very hospital. She played 'Miss Prism' and therefore on that occasion did not get to utter those infamous words – '*A handbag?*'

During my time there I had my own 'handbag' of course – a catheter which I would carry over my arm – (they only came in yellow though.)

Mr Steele went over the plan of action and on an August morning after a pre-med was administered, I sank into unconsciousness. I wasn't aware of much until the following day except that I was in a lot of pain. When I was ordered out into a chair while my bed was made I tried to explain that this was impossible, simply because I had no legs. (Lucky I went to the bank while I could).

The nurse explained it was because of the epidural I'd had for pain relief and that the feeling would come back in time.

"That's good," I said slipping to the floor.

When I did regain my legs, I tottered up and down the ward feeling a bit like a toy that's had some of its stuffing removed and been stitched up again. My daily goal was to reach the window facing out onto Frith Street.

Gradually of course, everything started working again. Clips were removed from the wound, leaving what would be a neat scar.

I left hospital and returned to everyday life, leaving

part of me behind for medical research. A few months later I received an envelope from Pennsylvania. Inside was the dollar equivalent of fifteen pounds and a letter from Janice who obviously decided to take the bus after all.

Apparently, I made it into *The Lancet* as the youngest woman to have undergone the operation. Fame at last.

Unfortunately, five years later, just when I thought it was safe to go back into the water, you might say, I was unlucky enough to have to make a return appearance to hospital again with a secondary tumour, this time on my lung.

I won't dwell on the operation or the fact that I am held together by staples even now. (I could never quite escape from office life even on the operating table). I can only say that pain aside, the worst part of being hospitalised for me was boredom. Being a 90 mph person, it was a complete nightmare to be thus incarcerated. I think it was the frustration and impatience that got me through it all. The collapse of my lung shortly after the operation and another being necessary to inflate it made my stay even longer than anticipated. The days would drag while I waited for the chest drains to stop bubbling, an indication that my lung was working on its own.

Six months of chemotherapy followed which meant one week out of four spent hooked up to drips. Talking of which, I found hospitalisation gave me time to reflect on my past relationships. They were very soon put into perspective, not that I would recommend this particular antidote to love affairs gone wrong.

By night, between bouts of vomiting as the chemo

ran through, I held a sort of vintage film festival in my head, revisiting scenes from my childhood just to concentrate on something other than feeling sick. Once, I found myself back in Twelve Acres playing in the snow as a kid. Back then my small world had been one of brilliant sunlit mornings, early dark, stoked up fires and hot water bottles hugged while frost patterned the bedroom windows. When snow fell I'd be one of several others heading out to make a snowman or to join the queue for the slide.

Another time I remembered being about twelve and there was snow again. I was wading through mounds of it in a pair of white 'kinky' boots purchased from my mother's catalogue. Emma Peel once wore a pair on *The Avengers* so these were a 'must have' even though they were useless in the snow. On my head I wore a white fur thingy which fastened with pom-poms under the chin. I reached the crossing gates at the end of the street where the steps were thickly white and was half way around 'the boards' (the section of Newtown Road that ran beside the railway works), when a blizzard blew up big time. Newtown became Antarctica as I persevered through the blinding snow, determined to reach my grandmother's flat. I hung onto someone's garden fence trying to get my breath and stay upright, but could barely see a yard ahead of me. Emma Peel was soon replaced by The Abominable Snowman when my hat became so heavy with snow that my neck ached from the weight of it. When my boots filled up it was all I could do to drag each foot along and I wondered if I should abandon them entirely. (In *The Avengers* Emma would no doubt have chosen a thigh-length variety for this job, probably stiletto heeled, never falling over once).

Eventually, I made it to my grandmother's flat. There was a blast of warmth as the door opened but no sign of 'Nan'. I remember how she defrosted me in front of her new gas fire and told me I was mad to have set out. I woke up and realised that she was no longer around. It would have been good to see her again, even for a moment.

On another occasion, I found myself back in primary school wandering the empty rooms doing a sort of inventory. It was raining when I arrived and the steamy vestibule where gabardine macs hung either side was puddled from an army of wet shoes.

The first room on the left with its pale green door was the infant's class and full of tiny desks and chairs. There was a smell of wooden floorboards, chalk, damp kids and the coke burning heater with a brass topped fireguard surrounding it. I remember the fear of my first day.

On the mantelpiece was a portrait of Our Lord wearing the crown of thorns. His eyes were in 3D – now open, now closed. It was a bit creepy for little kids but that's how it was at Catholic school back then – full on medieval.

On the wall was a picture of two rabbits playing in the grass and through the gothic shaped windows grey clouds rolled by. On the table in the corner were tins of powder paint in royal blue, red and yellow. In the cupboard behind teacher's desk were boxes of chalk, *Janet and John* books and dusters for the blackboard, which stood with its easel beside the door. Audible throughout was the constant sound of machinery from the neighbouring railway works.

Out in the hall, where the floor smelled of polish, the way it always did on the first day back after the holidays, a table had been put up for the mid-morning tuck shop. Cardboard boxes contained Potato Puffs, Jammy Dodgers, marshmallow biscuits and Wagon Wheels.

There was an altar with a statue of Our Lady on a white filigree cloth and on the wall above, a crucifix. To the right, on the floor, was the elephant's foot. Kids stood on this to be sung to when it was their birthday. Further along, to the left of the altar was the piano and behind that some bookshelves, screens and stacked dinner tables. These were set up every day for lunch and at Christmas were set close together to form a stage for the carol concert and nativity play. The caretaker would rig up a couple of curtains and it was all very exciting if you were taking part.

Looking back down the hall, a sink was situated in the left hand corner and a trolley full of plates scraped clean of leftover food from lunch. Two kids were chosen each day to perform this task before the trolley was then wheeled around to the kitchens for the grand washing up by the dinner ladies.

Straight ahead was the next class up from the infants', geared to kids around six or seven years old. Inside the tall cupboard beside the door, the first aid kit was kept. It's from here that Dettol was produced and plasters if anyone fell over. Behind the classroom door itself stood a cupboard containing jigsaw puzzles of religious scenes and countries of the world. These were done on Friday mornings when the priest occasionally dropped by and we had to leave off piecing together China and Japan or *The Last Supper* to stand for a blessing.

On the floor was the milk crate with a box of straws on the mantelpiece behind the heater. To the left of the door on the wall was a picture of the poem *As I Was Going to St Ives* in orange and black.

Turning left out of this room, past the sink, was a shadowy area where old toys were stored. There was a play oven and a few discoloured loaves of bread, a couple of rickety cots and several dolls that had lost eyes, arms or legs from years of handling. During my time there these ancient toys would eventually be replaced with 'the apparatus' – shiny new benches and nets of brightly coloured balls.

To the right was the classroom that I occupied at around eight or nine years old. Just inside the door was a bookshelf, then the heater. On the mantelpiece behind teacher's desk a vase of roses always stood. I located my own desk somewhere in the middle of the room. Inside lay a patterned wooden pencil case and a yellow exercise book marked 'Comprehension'. On the table beside teacher's desk toys were placed each Friday when we could bring in our favourite doll or car or annual. To the left of this a door led into the lobby and then out into the playground.

Across the hall, beyond the stacked tables was the last or 'leavers' classroom. Its glass windows faced into the hall giving the class teacher, the headmistress herself, the chance to keep an eye on all comings and goings. I turned the circular brass door handle and entered. The heater and fireguard were to the left of the door with the teacher's desk beyond. Behind this were shelves stacked with books. My own desk was towards the back of the class and opened easily enough to reveal coloured pencils, a fountain pen, a bottle of ink, a ruler for drawing margins, a 'Winkie' doll wearing earrings and a little red skirt. There were exercise books, another yellow one entitled 'Compositions'. Adjacent to my desk stood a high cupboard with books on top such as *The Water Babies*, *Ballet Shoes* and poems by Walter de la Mare.

Exiting through the door to the right of teacher's desk I found myself in the little vestibule where leaves had blown in from the lime trees outside. To the right was a small alcove in the wall, and to the left the lobby with a glass roof. More sodden leaves on the floor, more steamy macs.

Outside, beyond the low wall and chicken wire fence the nettle-covered bank sloped down to the railway yard and the building known as Shop 47.

To the right, in the corner beside a lime tree and an overhang of elderflower were the dustbins. The last one in the row of four had a rubber covered lid, good for sitting on in the height of summer as opposed to the others that scorched your legs.

Turning left and moving towards the end of the school yard, I passed through an alleyway hung with more elderflower leading back into the 'little ones'' playground. The weather had turned warm with sunlight slanting through. This then grew dazzling white until it became a nurse's apron and the factory noise became the rattle of the tea trolley on the Oncology Ward. The last bag dispensing chemo was done and I was exhausted as much from my nocturnal meanderings as from the treatment itself.

The horror all came to an end of course with the chemo having done its job miraculously leaving my hair intact. It was another strange experience of incarceration and a lesson being taught in how to appreciate your life. I thought I had been appreciating it over those five years and really didn't deserve that other bashing. In any case I survived, unlike poor Shop 47 which has since been demolished.

My mother always says that every cloud has a silver lining. I spent a lot of time waiting for the lining back then, but it eventually appeared a few weeks later in the form of Ian, that young man I may have passed at Dreamland. As we sailed off into the sunset with the horrors of my recent life left smouldering like the shark at the end of *Jaws*, I guess you could say the lining was definitely silver, if not gold.

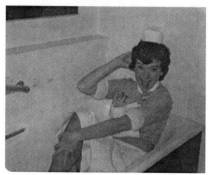

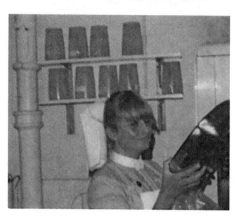

With nurses at the Middlesex 1980

Lovely old school alleyway

Shop 47 before its demise

PART TWO

THE STICKER

Having survived two bouts of serious illness it occurred to me that there was nothing I couldn't achieve if I put my mind to it. I therefore decided to enter that world of misfits, eccentrics, and general oddballs where I was convinced I would find a niche – in other words, the acting profession.

I made my stage debut with a local amateur dramatic company in Wellingborough where I was then living, as 'Kay' in *Out of Sight, Out of Murder*. The play was a thriller about an author whose characters all come to life in a thunderstorm. I was very nervous but mercifully no-one asked for their money back. Afterwards Betty, the director, made the mistake of suggesting I take up acting professionally.

It was my moment on the road to Damascus. Yes! This is the way to go, I told myself.

"Thank you, Betty," I simpered, all aglow. (If only she'd kept her trap shut I might have stayed relatively sane).

In the spring of 1987 I auditioned for the Guildford School of Acting, stumbling through Hermione from Shakespeare's *The Winter's Tale* and Stephanie from *Duet For One* by Tom Kempinski. The latter was based on the life of famous cellist, Jacquelyn du Prè, whose career was cut short due to multiple sclerosis. The first piece I did standing up, the second sitting down as the character was in a wheelchair, but that's probably the only distinction I made between the two, racked as I was with nerves. Even more horrifying was the prospect of singing in front of the audition panel.

"What are you going to perform for us?" enquired one member encouragingly.

"Er...*Bright Eyes*?" I offered, as though I had a whole repertoire up my sleeve if they'd asked for something else.

"Lovely."

You won't be saying that in a minute, I thought to myself as I plugged in my little tape recorder. Being musically illiterate, I had recruited my guitarist friend Gill to put together a backing track of the Simon and Garfunkel song so that I couldn't fail to know when to come in. The trouble was that my nerves caused me to pitch far too high with *'Is it a kind of dreeee-eeeeem?'* while Gill's gently-timed twanging went out of the window.

I waited for the panel to respond "Yes it is love, particularly in your case," but they only suggested I stop and try again, this time remembering to breathe as well as act the song. This was rather difficult unless you happened to be a cartoon rabbit. I made another attempt while gazing at the ceiling, imagining myself as a small, furry creature, bounding through the hedgerows.

A subdued silence followed and then a polite "thank you."

I made for the exit, only to have to return again shortly after to unplug my tape recorder. (Embarrassment factor – high).

Afterwards, I joined the other auditionees in a movement exercise which involved crossing the room in an imaginative way to piano music. I fell back on the grand jetés I'd performed as a child when inflicting my ballet routines on the audience at the primary school concerts. (Mercifully, the Friday afternoon entertainment was performed on the floor and not on those stacked tables or I may not have survived to tell the tale.) I also fell back onto the piano when an awkward chap in front of me prepared to launch himself like Billy Elliot does in *Swan Lake* at the end of the film. He flexed himself so far backwards that his head was almost under my chin before he took off. The studio not being very wide, I made the mistake of assuming there was room for one more jeté and hit the wall with my knee before skipping back for more, an eager smile hiding my pain.

I limped off at the end of the audition certain that I'd seen the last of Guildford. Of course it never pays to be too sure of anything and it was while temping in the Antiquities Department at the British Library several weeks later that I made the phone call and was told I'd been accepted. I took a walk around the mummies to calm myself.

With fees to save for, I started temping in earnest, working as many hours as possible to make up the shortfall from my grant. I got a job with an events management company based at the bottom of the Haymarket. Late one afternoon, I found myself alone in the office, the rest of the staff having departed for a huge exhibition in Beijing. I was just coming out of the loo when I noticed that the stairway leading down to the basement appeared to be full of smoke. I waste no time in dialling 999 already hearing my boss's commendation for saving the building from becoming a towering inferno in his absence. I could also hear the sound of fire engines in the distance. How efficient are our emergency services I thought to myself! Meanwhile, to my surprise, a workman appeared from the stairway below, covered in wood chippings.

"Quick!" I yelled, pointing to the street door. "This way!"

"Eh?" said the workman clearly unruffled.

"Smoke! Something's on fire down there!" I indicated the stairs from whence he'd come.

"Oh, that's not smoke, love," he informed me with a smile. "That's dust. I'm planing some wooden planks down in the basement. The guvnor arranged for me to come in and repair the floorboards while they're all away."

The fire sirens having becoming increasingly louder were now making their way down the Haymarket – three of them, big, red and shiny. In seconds they were outside with the fire crew shoving on helmets and running inside looking for where to aim the hoses.

"It's not a simple as that," said the disgruntled fire chief a few minutes later after I'd explained my mistake and a small crowd had gathered on the pavement. Just as every cloud has a silver lining, every call had to be recorded and he'd produced a clip board.

The firemen wound up the hoses, having no doubt decided where they'd like to aim them. The workman returned downstairs after doing a gesture to the fire chief which involved pointing to the side of his head and then to me. I scribbled my name where the fire chief indicated on his official looking form, disguising it as best I could in case I should be placed on police records as an emergency services' time waster. I sloped away as the engines move off, my face a-flame, if nothing else.

On another evening, after 'a long day's journey into night' spent temping, I hurried onto a train at Euston Station bound for home, or so I thought. It was only after I'd collapsed into my seat as the train pulled out, that the ticket inspector told me we would not be stopping at Wellingborough.

In no mood for games I explained that Wellingborough had obviously been advertised on the information board or I would not have got on in the first place. However, the inspector took great pride in assuring me that I was mistaken. The first stop would be Leicester and he could not tell me when there would be a train back to Wellingborough should one even exist.

'Only to be used in an emergency' stated the notice above the communication cord. Well, it was an emergency as far as I was concerned. I'd been working like a slave and I just wanted to get home as soon as possible.

When I recognised the sign for the Weetabix factory, an indication that we were approaching Wellingborough, I got up and pulled the cord.

Although I knew I was in potentially very serious trouble, it was actually quite exciting to hear the screech of brakes as the great steel monster began to slow down at my behest. This was shortly followed by the sound of voices and rushing feet. I moved out into the corridor to await my fate.

"It was me," I confessed to the ticket inspector sheepishly as he and the guard hurried past in search of the emergency. "You see, I have to get off here."

Just like the train a few minutes before, the two railwaymen now screeched to a halt like cartoon Tom and Jerry.

I explained to the guard (incredulous) how I was sure the train was to stop at Wellingborough and how the ticket inspector (furious) had told me otherwise. I apologised for any inconvenience caused. As a matter of fact it was quite satisfying to be able to say this to rail employees for a change instead of them saying it to me, as had often been the case during my many years as a commuter.

My sentence hung in the air – death by ticket machine or even worse, a hefty on the spot fine.

The guard phoned through to the stationmaster as it was to him that I had to report apparently. I could see this might be in danger of going legal so I resorted to tears and confusion. The guard looked sympathetic. The inspector did not.

"Oh, just get her off of here," he said crossly.

Honestly, what a fuss!

The guard wrestled with the door and by sheer luck, a bit of judgement and the assistance of Weetabix we appeared to have only overshot the platform by twelve feet or so. Not bad, considering (don't ask me to do it again though).

Someone brought a ladder and a lamp as it was turning a bit foggy. For a moment, the eerie siding was reminiscent of Dickens' *The Signalman*. *('Lookout! Below there!...)*. This was no time to wax lyrical though. I was wanted in the stationmaster's office immediately. With me safely on the platform, the inspector snapped the window back up. I couldn't see his face in the gloom but I expect it was as red as a stop light.

In a performance worthy of an Academy nomination at least, I shakily explained to the stationmaster the events that led to the train grinding to a halt and my terror of being stranded.

"I'm sure it said Wellingborough on the board in London. I'm so sorry!" I sniffed.

"Well, as luck would have it, you were right," said the kindly stationmaster in a manner not unlike that of Bernard Cribbins as Mr Perks in *The Railway Children*.

I left off dabbing my eyes and turned a bit *Bambi*.

"I was?"

"Yes. I've checked with London and apparently, Wellingborough was listed on the stops to begin with, but it must have been deleted after you had boarded."

"I knew it!" I exclaimed triumphantly.

Mr Perks then went on to gently warn me that all this aside it really wasn't a good idea to stop trains. However, for a young lady to be stranded late at night due to a misunderstanding with the railway was also not good (more eye dabbing from me) so we'd say no more about it.

I assured him that I would not be making a habit of it and with more sniffing and dabbing and apologising scuttled off to my car.

And the BAFTA goes to...

A Nervous Disposition

It was late afternoon on a snowy Friday in January 1987. Finishing up at my temp job, I gazed down into Carnaby Street below at shoppers hurrying through the slush. My boss, Miles was going away for the weekend and had nipped up to the flat he rented at the top of the building to get his stuff.

"See you on Monday," he said as I got ready to leave.

I called into the loo on the way downstairs, wrestling with the buttons on my sheepskin coat in preparation for the conditions outside. On my feet I sported a pair of fur-lined, crepe-soled boots, which although ungainly and extremely hot when travelling in the Underground were toastie in the snow. The look wasn't exactly Julie Christie in *Doctor Zhivago*, but I thought it unlikely that the fashion police would be out in those temperatures. Picking up my weekend groceries, I made for the front door, only to find it locked.

A horrible thought lurked somewhere in the back of my mind, but I wasn't going there – not yet anyway. Instead, I dumped my shopping, took a few deep breaths and returned upstairs, past the empty offices (only temps hang around late as every hour counts) on the first and second floors with "See you on Monday" ringing in my head.

I legged it up to the third floor, or as far as it was possible to leg it, swathed in heavy sheepskin. The staircase leading up to Miles's flat and the fire escape beyond was almost too narrow for my feet, now simmering away in those increasingly toastie boots. A door became visible half way up on the left, but my banging on it, at first tentatively and then quite desperately brought no reply. The awful truth was staring me in the face, but still I refused to admit that Miles, now on his way to his car, would shortly be Miles miles away.

It was 1987 B.M. (before mobiles). The offices were all locked until the cleaners arrived in the early morning. I'd often passed them on their way out around eight-thirty. Would I survive until then? I had food at least. Thank God for M and S, I thought to myself – Hang on a minute though, it's Friday. Perhaps the cleaners don't come on Saturdays. Maybe they won't arrive until Monday morning which means I could be here for the whole weekend! It didn't bear thinking about. Talking of bears, I caught sight of myself in the glass door to the office on the second floor looking like something out of *Grizzly Adams*. But there was no time to dwell on my appearance. I had to get out.

Back I went to the front door. It was ancient, like the one leading to Scrooge's chambers in *A Christmas Carol*. However, no face of Jacob Marley appeared in the gathering gloom, only a sturdy deadlock. The letter box lid was on a spring and I eventually managed to prize it open with the end of my comb. Clutching it painfully in my fingertips, I lowered my mouth and was about to give my own performance of Samuel Beckett's play, *Not I*, (a lone mouth speaking in the dark) in an attempt to call for help, when the futility of this exercise at last dawned on me. Should I even have managed to attract the attention of a passer-by, the chances of them having an exact replica of the required door key about their person were pretty slim – in fact they were probably a zillion to one against. Ah, but they could fetch help – the police, the fire brigade – (maybe not the fire brigade, my track record with them being less than favourable after that business in the Haymarket). The decision, like the letterbox, was taken out of my hands. The sound echoed in the shadowy hallway.

Do the lights go off automatically at some point? I wondered.

'Not suitable for people of a nervous disposition...'. This phrase was often used on TV in the 60s ahead of a spooky play. What if I was one of those people? No, I couldn't be. After all, I sat through a whole series of *Mystery and Imagination* when I was a kid, don't forget including, *The Tractate Middoth* a terrifying tale about a librarian in Victorian times haunted by a dead man with a spider hanging from his forelock. I couldn't bring myself to go into Ashford Library in the late afternoon for some time after that. I'd often laughed at the terror I felt back then, only to have it revived in that gloomy hallway as it grew increasingly darker.

The stairway, occupied by day with people going about their business, now took on a sinister aspect. The building was old. Perhaps it was haunted. Perhaps previous occupants were peering at me over the banisters at that very moment, each one with a spider dangling – Get a grip, I told myself. There has to be a way...

I remembered the fire escape door at the top of the narrow stairway past Miles' flat. It was just possible...

I picked up my shopping and tramped upstairs once again, trying not to look down into the stairwell.

'People of a nervous disposition...'

Sweat poured off of me as I reached the fire escape door with its push-bar. Mercifully, it opened and I walked out to find myself in a delightful Dickensian scene of rooftops and chimneys in the falling snow! However, this was no time to stop and admire the scenery. I peered over the parapet with a view to attracting the attention of passers-by. If a fire engine could be summoned I would simply give a false name – that was the answer.

'But soft! What light from yonder window breaks?' Shakespeare himself seemed to be on my side as I noticed a glow emanating from the adjacent building. I carefully inched along, clutching the parapet in one hand, my shopping in the other. Precarious as the transfer from one building to the next might be, I didn't want to have to go back for my groceries should I be fortunate enough to find an escape route.

The roof was quite slippery in the snow. Thank

goodness for those crêpe-soled booties, that's all I can say.

'Don't look down,' I told myself as I traversed the little walkway that linked the two buildings. Hey, what a good title for a film! Whereas *Don't Look Now* had a dwarf in a duffle coat running around Venice, I was starring in my own feature up there as a woman in sheepskin haunting the rooftops of Soho.

Once across, I moved carefully towards the source of light. It turned out to be coming from an office in which some sort of meeting was under way. Several executives were seated round a table. Being Friday evening, they'd got a bottle of wine on the go. One chap picked up his glass and took a sip when his eyes locked with mine. His face froze. I can't think why. What was so unusual about a woman appearing at a rooftop window in a blizzard dressed as Nanouk of the North carrying two bags of shopping?

They all eventually rushed to my aid. While one chap held up the ancient sash, I explained my predicament, joking that I didn't usually take this particular short cut back from Marks and Sparks. There were sympathetic – (at least I think they were sympathetic) – murmurs as I was helped, one slushy-booted foot at a time, through the window and across the smart sofa beneath. The carpet was only slightly smeared when my crêpe heel encountered an individual fruit trifle that had escaped from the shopping bag.

Thanking my rescuers profusely, I made for the door.

One offered to see me downstairs but I replied that I'd taken up enough of their time already and left them to their meeting. I hurriedly descended into the street wondering whether I would feature in the minutes under Matters Arising or Any Other Business.

My favourite parapet

It was a hot summer morning and I'd been up and down Piccadilly hunting in vain for a door number that didn't seem to exist. I eventually found a phone box and dialled the firm I was to temp for.

"We're in Piccadilly," a voice replied when I asked for directions.

"Yes, but which side?"

The phone box was like a sauna and the balance on my phone card (then the latest way of using a public telephone) was rapidly heading downwards from 'six'.

"Hang on. I'm new here," came the response. "I'll just check,"

Three…

"Hello?"

Two, One…

"We're on the same side as…"

Zero.

Oh, well who needs a job anyway? I asked myself.

I thought of how much I still needed to save for my drama school fees and decided that I did.

I crossed the road in the direction of a tobacconist's for another phone card. Passing a travel shop, I gazed at a poster of deserted beach and a sparkling turquoise sea, imagining myself strolling along the white sand with the breeze blowing through my hair. In reality it was stuck to my face with sweat and I would shortly be sporting a huge blister on my heel where my slingback rubbed. Instead of the cry of sea birds, there was only the din of traffic until a cabbie yelled at someone to 'Fuck awf'.

The beach scene came to an abrupt halt at the end of the window and there on a brass plate was the number I'd been looking for. I'd arrived.

"You couldn't have been reading the numbers right," said Doris, the office manageress in reply to my excuse for being late. "It's quite simple really."

Doris, who had obviously made the journey every day for the last two hundred years, went on to boost my morale even further by informing me that temps weren't welcome as a rule. "We don't like agencies," she said hurrying me down a corridor leading to God knows where. "He moans about the cost, I can tell you."

"He" was Mr Bell, boss of the small legal practice.

We finally reached our destination, a small, stuffy office facing out onto a church and a small yard below.

"You're there," said Doris, pointing to a desk upon which stood a typewriter and a pile of files. "He likes two copies of everything. Tea and coffee is in the kitchen opposite and the ladies' is down the end of the corridor. There's no overtime – nine to five, right?" with that, she turned on the heel of her Hush Puppy and was gone.

At a desk beside the window sat a large woman with bobbed black hair and round glasses. Her puffed sleeved dress gave her the look of an oversized schoolgirl as she hammered away at the typewriter. She didn't stop until Doris was well out of earshot and then paused briefly to introduce herself as Tanya Bean.

"He's a real beast," she said of the boss. "I've been here a month and he's had me in tears twice. He's so sarcastic you wouldn't believe it! Just wait till you hear those tapes, I've never heard anything like it in my life! He's gone through two girls this week. They couldn't stick it. I'm only here for the money."

Aren't we all? I thought as I sat down, stuck the first tape into the dictaphone and tuned in.

I saw in my mind's eye an elderly man dozing fitfully, waking every so often to dictate a few incoherent words. From the loud squeaking in the background, I assumed that he worked from home, in his conservatory perhaps, where a tropical bird swung to and fro, joining in every so often with his master's voice.

The chap obviously had a lisp but that wasn't the main problem. The coming and going of his voice was like the reception I got on that transistor I had in my teens. I rewound the tape several times until phrases like 'poth-eth', 'wathing knife n' up', 'Mith Reline', and 'In plimtholth' started to take on a familiar pattern, but I was nowhere nearer solving their meaning. I decided to do each letter in draft form and left spaces for Mr Bell to fill in. Unfortunately, there was more white space than anything else.

On returning from the kitchen where I'd got a second cup of tea and a frown from Doris, I was informed in a frenzied whisper by Tanya that Mr Bell had entered the building. She then began bashing even harder. I was anxious yet fascinated at the prospect of meeting the owner of the sleepy voice and Polly the parrot.

The door opened and Mr Bell shuffled into the room. He was old and lop-sided in a suit shiny from wear. He sported bifocals and his lower lip protruded slightly, giving him a vague look of Churchill. Tanya's face froze as he made straight for her desk.

"No, no, no, you thilly creature!" he exclaimed as he scored his dissatisfaction across her work. "Thank God my grandchild'th a boy!"

He turned out of the room tutting.

"Told you," whimpered Tanya, removing her specs to dab at her eyes with a tissue.

I thought Mr Bell hadn't noticed me and that I could slip down into the street with him being none the wiser when the intercom on my desk buzzed loudly.

"Young woman, where are my letterth?" he enquired. "I left a tape on your dethk thith morning, what'th devilth the hold up?"

"Yes, yes. I'll bring them in," I replied

I picked up the signature book and headed into the corridor. There was still time to turn left and escape, but I had my drama school fees to think of. Mr Bell couldn't be allowed to stand in my way. Gritting my teeth I turned right. Standing at the doorway to his office, I didn't see him at first, secreted as he was behind several columns of files.

"What are you thtanding there for? Come in, thilly and take a theat," instructed one of the columns.

I moved into the room and sat. It was then that I became conscious of something moving about the floor beneath the great old desk. I looked down to see a pin-striped bottom.

"Darren, haven't you found that paper yet? I needed to work on it thith afternoon for goodneth thake!"

"It's not here," replied Darren, Articles Clerk and owner of the bottom. "You must have left it in court."

"I thertainly did not and don't be tho bluddy cheeky," replied Mr Bell grabbing the signature book and handing me another tape.

"Do thith one nextht. It'th very urgent."

I returned to the office but had barely reached my desk when the intercom buzzed again.

"Thith ith an utter thambawth," said Mr Bell of my endeavours. "Come back here immediately and bring a gun. I'm going to thoot you!"

"See!" hissed Tanya, taking a forkful of her lunch from her top drawer and closing it again quickly so that the air was permeated with tuna and onion. "He's a pig!"

"Re-type everything!" demanded Mr Bell as I returned to his sanctum. "I want it by three o'clock and no thlacking!"

I headed back out, avoiding Darren as he emerged, mole-like, from beneath a mountain of paperwork near the door.

I'd been working for a while without interruption. Just when I began to think that this might be a good sign, the intercom buzzed.

"Yes, Mr Bell?" I answered politely.

"I've got a crothbow and you are in my thighth, believe me."

During the ensuing days I battled with Mr Bell's incoherent meanderings until eventually they started to take on a vague pattern. I began to achieve a sense of satisfaction at turning tape after tape into recognizable English. Apparently Mr Bell was handling a property matter for a firm based in Greece.

'Wathing knife n'up' became washing(hyphen)up when the use of kitchen facilities was in question. 'Potheth' turned out to be 'Apostrophe S', 'Mith Reline' was 'miss three lines' and 'Plimtholl' became 'Limassol' – easy when you knew how.

When my efforts were acceptable they were met with silence and when they weren't that infernal buzzer would go and I'd get an ear-bashing ranging from "Thtart running before I take aim" to "I'm giving thith to my grandthon to re-type, he'll do a better job."

One morning the message was "Lithen carefully. I'm ithooing protheedingth for murder..."

I couldn't help but feel excited by the prospect of graduating from property maintenance to something so interesting. Flattered that Mr Bell should have trusted me with such confidential information, I glanced triumphantly at Tanya.

"Yourth," says Mr Bell before clicking off.

My smile froze as I wound the next sheet of paper into the typewriter.

One morning I was summoned in for dictation and had taken down about three letters in shorthand from Mr Bell, who lay slumped in his chair

"Another letter to the thame thilly thod," he mumbled into his shirt front. When he began swiveling from left to right, the source of the squeaking on the tape was revealed – his chair needed a drop of 'Three-in One' oil. The picture of Mr Bell working in his leafy conservatory vanished as did Polly the parrot.

"Got all that, mith?" asked Mr Bell eventually.

"Yes. Is that all for now?" I enquired hopefully, feeling as though my arm was about to drop off.

He replied, as he often did when asked a question with "Read my lipth".

I tried but there was nothing much to read apart from a bubble of saliva and a crumb from lunch.

All good things must come to an end. Eventually I was informed by Doris that a permanent secretary had been found for Mr Bell and my services were no longer required. Tanya kept in touch for a while and I learned that my replacement, a male, rolled cigarettes and smoked them out of the window all day, much to her annoyance. Darren departed shortly after me with a back injury, probably as a result of so much scrabbling under the desk.

As for Mr Bell, I encountered him just once more in Piccadilly one afternoon a few weeks later, dawdling across the road lugging his ancient briefcase. The bus was almost upon him before he saw it and the blast from its hooter sent him scurrying towards the pavement. The driver yelled furiously out of the window. I couldn't quite hear what he was saying, but I could read his lips.

The Sticker in Training

On a September morning in 1987, I found myself sitting with a crowd of other students in Guildford's Bellerby Theatre, once known as the Bellairs Playhouse. After a welcome by the principal, we received a lecture from one of the teachers on 'Stickers and Quitters'. Stickers were those who would see the course out and give it everything they'd got. These students, the teacher assured us, would reap the benefit of all the school had to offer. Quitters – those who would give up – were not even worth thinking about as far as I was concerned because the title 'Quitter' would never apply to me, that was for sure. I was going to give this two hundred per cent. I was a Sticker through and through.

There was great emphasis on physicality, as you might expect. Mondays kicked off with a rigorous exercise class, just in case we'd all become a bit too relaxed over the weekend. There was ballet, tap and historical (often hysterical when we went wrong) dance, including the Elizabethan pavan and elegant routines from the Restoration period involving masks and fans

The tap class was hard work and to get any kind of tapping sound was difficult if, like me, you didn't have the right sort of feet, let alone shoes. The best tappers had high insteps and could shuffle-ball-change in an instant, whereas I was always a beat behind, still shuffling when others were changing. Ballet was reasonably OK – I remembered the basics from my childhood lessons. Nevertheless, I still tended to overestimate the number of jetés possible in any given space.

I noticed that Daniel, the stiff-looking boy I'd encountered at the audition never seemed to derive much pleasure from being at the school at all. Although well spoken, he did not appear well provided for. Even though most of us were living on shoestrings, Daniel seemed to spend all his days in abject poverty. After being spotted picking up dog-ends and borrowing money here and there, the poor boy soon became something of a joke. I felt quite sorry until I was partnered with him for fencing and stage fighting. Clearly a method actor, Daniel believed in doing it for real. Once, during Rapier and Dagger, he managed to slice through my tights, drawing blood. Defending myself, I caught him a glancing blow on the back of his hand. Needless to say, when the time came we failed the stage fighting exam, our marks being too insignificant, (unlike the marks we had inflicted on each other).

For mask work, we all had to bring in a mask representing a creature totally opposite to our own physical type. My mask was a cow and I lumbered about as heavily as I could in it instead of speeding along as usual. People went to a lot of trouble over their masks – cats, dogs, elephants and even a turtle moved blindly around the floor. Daniel's mask was a cornflake packet with eyeholes in, so goodness knows how he usually viewed himself if this was intended to display the opposite.

The study of stagecraft involved being alert and sensitive to those around you in a given space. Friday morning's class was geared towards this in addition to the creating and controlling of energy. The idea was to 'unleash the tiger inside us and ride it'. This involved moving around the room, slowly at first, then gradually building up speed until we were all throwing ourselves about in a sweaty frenzy.

Once this heightened state had been reached, we were to use the energy to achieve maximum concentration and focus. We then began to pass sticks to each other. Having caught someone's eye, (not with the stick, although it was a close thing once or twice), we then had to anticipate when to exchange sticks, thereby building the trust of our fellow actors.

The session ended with all of us lying on the floor in total relaxation. During this time, I would often find myself gazing up at the rafters trying not to slip into unconsciousness.

Another exercise in building trust involved us all standing bunched together as tightly as possible with our eyes closed. Gradually, we'd all begin swaying at the same time, like one living organism. During this exercise, I've found it imperative to not to be positioned anywhere near a stocky chap called Oliver whose laugh was like that of Muttley from the TV cartoon *Dastardly and Muttley*. If I heard him squeaking I'd have to grit my teeth and look at the floor as to be caught giggling, or 'corpsing' as it is known in the theatre, was unforgiveable. We had to remember at all times that we were training to be professionals and to behave as such. It was just bad luck that one day when we were in the huddle I caught sight of Oliver in the mirror, grinning like a Halloween lantern. I tried to stifle a snigger, but soon the group, which up until then had been swaying gently, like a great sea anemone became more like a bouncy castle.

Voice work while being of prime importance, was I have to admit, among the most boring of classes as far as I was concerned. Others were mime and Laban. (I often found myself yawning while pushing my hands against an imaginary pane of glass or stretching my arms beyond the universe.) One day, during a voice projection class in the mirrored studio, I was reciting a passage from *King Lear* with Richard, another almighty giggler. In order to 'hit the back wall' the tutor suggested we stand on chairs during the speech. This we duly did while the rest of the class, including Oliver, looked on. The first line, *'Blow, winds, and crack your cheeks! rage! blow!'* needless to say was a recipe for disaster. Muttley was soon loose, shoulders shaking, while Richard and I gave up all attempts at self control and just stood there laughing our heads off. Our tutor, who only a few days before had congratulated me on my reading of an excerpt from *The Picture of Dorian Gray*, now looked as though she despaired of me entirely.

We were lucky enough to study Shakespeare with the now late Sheila Moriarty. Sheila illustrated each lesson with anecdotes from her many years in the profession encouraging us to be bold in performance and push the boundaries. "I'd rather pull you off the ceiling than scrape you off the floor," was her motto. Sheila had a wonderful way of simplifying Shakespearean plots and bringing them up to date in a way you could identify with. You felt that you were in the presence of someone quite unique whose words really were pearls of wisdom.

We went on to study the Restoration era. Our tutor was an oracle about the period and crammed us with so much information that on following Oliver out of class one day I asked why his head was on one side. He replied that it was heavy with so much knowledge.

We worked on plays of the time such as *The Country Wife* (1670) and *The Man of Mode* (1676) which were performed in the re-opened playhouses after Cromwell's demise. Having had a brush with the Cromwellian look myself in the past, I studied the charming costumes worn by ladies during the reign of King Charles II. The boys wore frock coats and bowed with a flourish, while we girls put ringlets in our hair and wore pearls around our necks. We carried fans and tied panniers beneath our skirts to make them stick out. I liked to imagine my own ancestors wearing these elegant togs, but of course this is highly unlikely. While Aphra Benn who was born in Wye, near Ashford penned *The Rover*, her famous play of the period, my ancestors were probably labouring in the fields nearby, in clothes suitable for that occupation.

Our production of *Cider With Rosie* was interesting to say the least. As Miss Crabbe, the village schoolmistress, I was to be placed on the mantelpiece just before the interval by the naughtiest boy in class. Art imitated life when the role of Spadge Hopkins was given to none other than Oliver, who was also doubling up as the village baker. There was more doubling up when we discovered that the mantelpiece had been built way too high and Oliver, dressed in braces and short trousers, struggled red-faced to place me there. On the afternoon of the performance, he just about managed it and I hung on like grim death until the blackout at the end of the scene when I slid to the floor in a heap.

During the second act, the atmosphere out front sounded tranquil from the dressing room as Mrs Lee and her family reclined around the picnic basket to the tweeting of birds and the baa-ing of sheep. Daniel, imminently due on, began frantically trying to unpick a knot in his bootlace. I lent a hand but the knot refused to budge. As his entrance cue drew ever nearer, Daniel had no option but to try and force his foot into the boot through the small hole left by the unforgiving lace. This resulted in it getting stuck half in and half out of the boot.

"It's no good! I'll have to go on as I am!" exclaimed Daniel as his cue came and went. Out he hopped – the first of Laurie Lee's brothers to have a club foot.

As 'Crabby'with Spadge Hopkins

With fellow giggler, Richard

Graduation Day with Rik Mayall

Digs

While I studied drama by day, there was quite a bit of it going on out of hours, at least as far as my digs were concerned. The advert I answered for a room to rent not far from school sounded perfect until I moved in and realised that my landlady, Annabel was slightly unhinged with an alcoholic boyfriend. Late at night she would be waiting up for me, eager to relate the latest episode in her disastrous relationship. Experienced in disastrous relationships, I could sympathise. However, a Sticker's day was full on and all I wanted to do was conk out.

One afternoon I came home to find the front door wide open, the radio blaring and Annabel nowhere to be seen. She returned late in the evening slightly the worse for wear, having nipped down town for something – she couldn't quite remember what. Mercifully, there was no sign of lover boy Tom, who tended to turn up in the early hours hammering on the door, often quite hammered himself. Annabel charged into my room to relate how she and her friend had been dancing on tables in a bar in the high street. I had to admire my landlady. She was no chicken but certainly knew how to party.

I woke just before dawn one Tuesday morning to much yelling and slamming of doors. It was clear that

Annabel had a visitor of the drunken boyfriend kind. I got ready to skedaddle. Tuesday's were hard enough already, due to an hour of musical theatre which involved individual singing. I'd expanded my repertoire from *Bright Eyes* to include *Sing a Rainbow* made famous by Cilla Black in 1966, about to be made tortuous by me in 1987 for those on the receiving end. I planned to head off to a workman's cafe for breakfast and to prepare for the ordeal ahead.

I crept downstairs a little too late. Through the glass panelled door of the dining room I was surprised to see Tom's silhouette. I was even more surprised on opening the door to see that he had apparently mistaken the dining room table for the toilet. At singing class I was unable to sing a rainbow of any colour, having already spotted a bright yellow one where I usually eat my cornflakes (lucky it wasn't Co-Co Pops).

I left Annabel's abode soon afterwards due to her life being far too theatrical even for me.

The next establishment had its drawbacks too.

"You just caught me before I got started!" laughed the young man at the cottage door who introduced himself as Ray. With his mop of dark curls, yellow vest and denim jacket, he looked like a children's entertainer or a possible candidate for the lead in *Godspell*.

"I hope I'm not interrupting anything," I said, noticing an artist's paintbrush in his hand.

"No, not at all," answered Ray, gesturing for me to enter . "I was just playing around with ideas."

The cottage was situated down a winding lane off the beaten track. Somewhere a couple of dogs were barking. Their owner was barking too, but of course I didn't know that at the time, being taken in by the David Essex look and the paintbrush. I followed him into the sitting room where a sketch of Michael Caine lay on the floor.

"Just working on a portrait of Michael," Ray informed me, suggesting that he was on first name terms with the star.

When I asked who else lived in the house, Ray explained that he had been alone since his girlfriend moved out a few weeks before. The decision to split, he insisted was entirely mutual. Both need more space – Ray for his painting and Janie from Ray as I would discover.

"What an arty house we'll have!" he quipped. "Me painting and you acting!"

"Yes!" I agreed as he showed me the room I was to occupy. The view from the window was of golden fields on a sunny October morning. There will certainly be peace and quiet here, I reasoned, handing over the deposit.

Unloading my belongings took several trips from the car. I was up and down the stairs a dozen times with clothing, shoes, bedding, books, plays and the bedside lamp made from a Mateus Rose bottle that I'd had since the Oval flat. Throughout this operation, Ray stood watching with his arms folded. A scene from *Psycho* flashed through my mind – the bit when Janet Kerr first arrives at the motel and Norman Bates watches her every move. Silly! I told myself. Being an artist, perhaps assisting with the lugging of my belongings upstairs would have impeded the flow of Ray's creative energy.

Once moved in I was so busy at school that I didn't see much of my landlord. Apparently going through his 'blue' period, he'd fitted bulbs of this colour in all of the downstairs rooms, apart from the kitchen where a faulty strip light intermittently flickered on and off like in a David Lynch movie. Ray didn't possess a television and seemed to spend his evenings in the blue shadowy living room not doing very much at all. To come across him sitting in there on the occasions I returned late in the evening was a bit unnerving to say the least.

Ray's bedroom, which I once peeked at while he was out and then only from the safety of the doorway, was a shambles – its lack of aesthetic charm not improved by the presence of a murky tank full of large terrapins. I once knew a girl who admitted to keeping a couple of snakes in a cage at the foot of her bed. Their diet, she explained, was dead mice, a supply of which would be delivered every so often, packed in ice to be thawed out on her radiators. She assured me that snakes make ideal pets once you get past their overall appearance. I assured her in turn that I could never get past it. Anyone who is content to sleep with reptiles at the foot of their bed has something wrong with them as far as I'm concerned, even if they appear normal.

One morning I woke to the sound of a car screeching to a halt, followed shortly after by a pair of high heels tipping along the path. A loud rapping on the door set the dogs barking and Ray stumbling downstairs. An altercation followed during which Ray seemed to be pleading with the female visitor. Her response included phrases like "when hell freezes over" and "fucking arsehole".

"Could I have heard Janie earlier?" I asked Ray in the kitchen after the woman had driven away like a bat out of hell.

"Oh...er...yes," he smiled. "She just popped in to say hello and pick up a few things."

I suggested that the dogs might need to go out. It was difficult enough to prepare any food in a kitchen reeking of disinfectant and cleared up doo-doo, let alone with the poor things rubbing around my legs in desperation.

"They're Janie's," replied Ray. "But she says she doesn't want them."

In retaliation for Janie's refusal to take himself or the two wire-haired mongrels back into her life, Ray decided from then on to restrict the dogs' walks even further. He proceeded to slip into a general state of depression and I returned to find even more whoopsies on the floor with 'Blue Ray' surly and uncommunicative. He stopped shaving and the happy- go- lucky David Essex of *Godspell* was soon replaced by Jack Nicholson in *The Shining*.

One night in October, the wind started cutting up rough, building to gale force. Returning to the remote cottage and its occupant was suddenly a daunting prospect. I scuttled up to my room in case he should loom up from the shadows like the Monster from the Black – or even the Blue Lagoon.

I woke in the early hours to the wind screaming like a banshee and something repeatedly hitting the window. Ray's cottage had turned into *Wuthering Heights* as bits of tree were flung against the house. Outside, whole branches rolled along the fields like giant tumbleweeds. Downstairs the terrified dogs were yelping like mad. I was scared, but not scared enough to seek out Ray. The whole scenario was like a crazy nightmare as the tornado raged on through the night.

The storm eventually blew itself out and the morning dawned bright and sunny. The sound of chainsaws filled the air as fallen trees were cut and removed from across the lane. Ray was vigorously chopping a branch away from the garden fence with an axe, a look of rapt concentration on his face. On the way to school I picked up Richard, my comedy partner from the voice class who was standing optimistically at a bus stop. In his emerald green jacket and red suede shoes, he could have been an elf driven from his home by the overnight tempest. We exchanged stories about what would turn out to be the worst storm to hit England since 1703, with eighteen people dying from its effects.

The transport system was badly disrupted and my journey back by road after the following weekend was interminable. It was very late on the Sunday evening when I finally drew up outside the cottage. I was almost relieved when the blue light wasn't shining in the window, an indication that Ray had probably gone to bed. When I unlocked the back door and entered the kitchen I discovered that the electricity was out and there were no lights working at all. The dogs' barking was building to a crescendo and the smell was even worse than usual. I edged my way around the floor, hoping to avoid treading in anything and then felt my way upstairs to my room. I crept under the duvet and stayed there until it got light. Everything was a horrible blur until I realised I hadn't removed my contact lenses. (Doh!). Peering into Ray's room I saw that his bed, the usual unmade mess, had not been slept in and apart from the terrapins floating in their dark tank and the dogs downstairs, I was alone.

I packed my stuff, feeling bad about leaving the poor dogs and the terrapins to their fate as I drove away. In the best horror movies, Ray would now have emerged from behind my seat grinning maniacally in the rear view mirror. It was almost a comfort when on rounding a bend, I saw him speeding past me in the other direction. I thought about getting my deposit back, but the remembered the way he used that axe and just kept going.

The Sticker Released

Our final showcase at Drama School, a selection of vignettes by Strindberg entitled *Scenes from a Cynical Life* was held at the Young Vic Studio. I played a mad old duchess and enjoyed sweeping about in a long frock. My parents came to see the show which was a nice change from visiting me in hospital.

The diplomas on graduation day were presented by comedian and actor, Rik Mayall. A programme for the afternoon was put together to include all our mug shots. However, the facilities in the school's administration office weren't exactly high-tech, particularly the photocopier. My photograph came out so faintly that my features were barely discernible. Hamlet's words to Ophelia – *'God has given you one face, and you make yourself another'* sprang to mind when during the course of the morning I was summoned to draw in my own nose and mouth.

Our party that evening involved a cabaret, and those who fancied could do a turn. I joined a couple of others in a scene from *The Antiques Roadshow*. One of the 'precious' items brought in for consideration was a yellow money box shaped like a mouse with enormous ears. When I, as the expert broke the news that the item was worthless, a hopeful smile slipped from the owner's face and they kicked up a fuss (which of course never happens on TV) and the money box got dumped unceremoniously into the bin.

The evening, full of songs and sketches was rounded off by none other than Daniel. Usually so stiff and reserved, he decided to show a side to his character that up until then he'd preferred to keep hidden. The dimming of the lights was followed by a drum roll and then from between the curtains a single jackboot came into view followed by an expanse of skinny thigh in a fishnet stocking. The rest of Daniel then emerged in a long trench coat. His hair was greased down, he wore ruby red lipstick and a monocle in his mascara-fringed eye. More camp than Millett's shop window, he slid out of the coat and began to serenade us Dietrich-like with *Falling in Love Again* while puffing away on a cigarette in a long, elegant holder. He then went more up tempo, launching into a medley from *Cabaret* while flexing his booted legs against our chairs á la Sally Bowles. It was Berlin, it was divine decadence, it was...Daniel?

After the party, we all said fond goodbyes with promises to keep in touch. There had been tears, frustrations and petty jealousies, particularly when anyone acquired those all-prized objects of desire, an audition or interest from an agent. There were love affairs, two of which culminated in weddings, there was the forging of several friendships that have stood the test of time.

A few weeks later I landed my first professional role as 'Lulu' in *Intimacy*, a two-hander adapted from a short story by Jean-Paul Sartre.

Directed by Michael Almaz of the Artaud Theatre Company, *Intimacy* was an ongoing piece of fringe theatre, the cast for which was changed every six weeks. After a tip off from the current Lulu, whose time in the role was almost up, I read the part with an actress named Carol who was to play opposite me as 'Rirette'. The 'theatre' was a converted upstairs room in a pub off Leicester Square – a typical arrangement on the fringe.

Also typical on the fringe, the dressing room, like the pay was almost non-existent, just a narrow space behind the performing area. While one of us was out front giving her all, the other struggled into her next costume a couple of feet away. In the play, set in Paris in the late 1940s Lulu is married to a big lump of a man called Henri who pays her no attention and is never actually seen. When Rirette persuades Lulu to run off with her lover, Pierre, she grabs a taxi and heads for the station, but it all goes wrong and she ends up staying with Henri after all.

We had reasonable houses at weekends – the curious being drawn in by the title, although parading about in suspenders and French knickers was about as intimate as it got. Audiences were sparse during the week and on one occasion only three people showed up, but being true Stickers we went on anyway.

I was always terrified of messing up and quite relieved when it was Carol rather than myself who appeared to make a slip one evening. The gaffe caused us to skip a couple of pages and I was quite proud of my quick thinking as I improvised like mad to get us back on track.

"We ought to see what went wrong," suggested a red-faced Carol afterwards, "so that it doesn't happen again."

"Oh, don't worry," I said reassuringly. "We all make mistakes. You'll be fine again tomorrow night."

"What do you mean?" replied Carol indignantly. "It was you that went wrong!"

"What?"

We sat down and went over the script – Quelle horreur! She was right! It was my fault after all that Lulu left Paris far sooner than she should have done, without even taking a taxi! As a consequence, the play was shortened by ten minutes. Luckily, the director didn't decide to look in on the show, or the fiver from the cash box might somehow have been overlooked at the end of that week.

I apologized profusely and sloped off to where I'd left my car. When it refused to start, due to the cold or damp or the fact that it was about twenty years old, I peered under the bonnet knowledgeably. This attracted a group of winos who started poking about with leads and things. The smell of alcohol mixed with petrol must have had some effect as the engine finally caught and I zoomed off leaving the winos waving behind me. I guess it had been one of those nights.

David

During and after the run of *Intimacy* I worked nearby for The Theatres' Trust, an organisation headed up by Director, John Earl and his colleague, David Cheshire. The Trust, which then occupied an attic in St Martin's Court, is dedicated to the conservation of theatres in the West End and throughout the UK. The work was very interesting and during my time with John and David, initial moves were made towards the restoring of the Lyceum in Covent Garden which eventually reopened in 1996.

As well as being concerned with research, David was leading authority on theatre architecture and music hall – (pity he missed my 'Old Tyme' debut in that butcher's apron). Part of my job was to type up his edits on the TTT newsletters. These were a mixture of reports and debates about theatre protection, design and conservation. I also helped David with his work on *Curtains!!!* the first gazetteer of British theatres, advising voluntary groups campaigning to reopen old theatres and also on *Theatrephile*, an illustrated journal.

For all his wisdom, David was a quiet and reserved fellow. During the Trust meetings he would sit taking minutes and was never asked for advice, in spite of probably knowing more about the theatres being discussed than anyone in the room. Only after his death in 2010 did I read the full extent of David's knowledge and expertise. He had worked in the theatre himself as a scene painter, scene-shifter and as an actor at Northampton Repertory Theatre, a place I often visited when I lived in that area. His dedicated research contributed to the restoration of the Old Vic, Sheffield Lyceum and Wimbledon Theatre. He wrote over 900 articles and encyclopaedia entries, for publications such as *The Stage* and *Theatre Quarterly*.

During my time at TTT, I was lucky enough to be given a copy of David's biography of Ellen Terry, to whom a museum is dedicated in Tenterden, near Ashford.

Whenever I pick up this book, I remember with fondness our chats and David's expert knowledge of the early London stage performers, such as Ellen Terry herself and Henry Irving after whom he named his two children. I'm proud to have known him.

David Cheshire 1935 – 2009

David Cheshire

Theo

While working at a film production and distribution company in Soho, I was introduced to Mr Theo Cowan. Theo had spent the greater part of his career as a publicist to the stars, but a less starry character it would be hard to find. Theo was a modest, unassuming gentleman. He worked tirelessly for his clients and was held in great esteem. Theo was friendly with the fellows that I worked for and often called in for a chat. He was always full of amusing anecdotes and had a policy never to take life to seriously.

We kept in touch over the years, and one September evening in 1991, arranged to have dinner. I pitch up at Theo's office, where he was rounding off his days' work. From a drawer he produced a sepia photograph of his younger self as a soldier in North Africa. Theo never revealed much about his earlier life, so I felt rather privileged to be shown this memento. As he got up from his chair, I noticed that Theo walked with the aid of a stick and was clearly not in the best of health. Typically, he made no reference to this as we walked to the garage in Poland Street where he always parked his stately old car.

After dinner, Theo dropped me at Kings Cross station. I wished him well and suggested we meet again soon.

On opening a copy of *The Stage* newspaper on my return from holiday a couple of weeks later, I was shocked and saddened to see Theo's obituary. He died the day after I last saw him, seated at his desk doing the work he so loved. I called round to his office where a colleague explained how, on having completed his latest project, Theo had given a sigh of contentment as though it was OK to go now.

On his desk where he and I had sat only a few days before, a vase of Stargazer lilies now stood.

The memorial service at the Church of St Martin-in-the-Fields on a cold day in November was attended by Theo's many friends in the industry. The actor, Jeremy Irons gave a remembrance and there was one hymn, *For The Beauty of the Earth*, but it was the closing song, *On the Sunny Side of the Street* that said everything about the Theo we would all remember.

I feel honoured to have known this remarkable man.

Theo Cowan 1918 – 1991

With Theo at Simpsons

I got to wear some gorgeous costumes when I played a Venetian countess in Don Taylor's *Daughters of Venice*, a role portrayed by the brilliant Frances Barber on BBC Radio. The countess leaves her infant daughter at a convent orphanage, returning to find her years later when she has become rich. Directed by dear Therese Kitchen of Quercus young people's theatre, we played for a week at the Wilde Theatre in Bracknell.

I was in great company with the fabulous actress Jean Marlow playing the Madre or Reverend Mother of the convent orphanage, and lovely Eamonn Jones as Mr Punch in the masked carnival scene. With a career stretching back to the fifties, Jean appeared in many films and television series such as *Z Cars*, *George and Mildred*, and *Dixon of Dock Green* to name but a few. She also played a nurse in the famous *Blood Donor* episode of *Hancock's Half Hour*. Eamonn appeared in such popular television favourites as *The Sweeney*, *London's Burning* and *The Bill* as well as many theatre productions.

I was lucky enough to work with Jean and Eamonn again a few months later in Therese's adaptation of *The Secret Garden* by Frances Hodgson Burnett. In this production I played 'Lilias', the ghost mother, and had to float about the garden quite a bit before ending up on a swing. During the performance week, I drove two hours there and back after the day job. Being totally knackered, it was a miracle I didn't sail from the swing into the audience and send it back empty. The Sticker remained in place however, and the show went on without a hitch.

I next applied to a children's touring theatre company with that obscure object of desire in mind, the Equity card.

At the audition I talked a bit about myself, how I had recently left drama school, the plays I had done and how in true Sticker fashion I was prepared to do anything any time anywhere no matter how far afield.

"How are you with mask?" asked the artistic director.

"Oh, no problem there!" I replied remembering the plastic cow exercise at Guildford. 'I really enjoy working with masks.'

"Try this one on for size," he said whipping out a Basil Brush woolly pull-on. Basil stared open mouthed, looking as surprised to see me as I was him.

"I'm not sure it will fit," I said, struggling to pull the thing over my head.

"They can be a bit tight, it's true," said the director's assistant. "But once you find the eyeholes, you've cracked it."

I stood sweating in the woolly darkness, tugging the thing this way and that in search of a glimmer of daylight. But the more I tugged the tighter and more stifling the mask became. I tried not to think about how many people had been there before me, who were perhaps not too fussy about hygiene and forced myself to concentrate on the Equity card. I found the eyeholes eventually, but they were a little too wide apart, so I had to manage with just the one.

"Say something," said the artistic director, a distant blur.

"Yes," said his assistant. "Say a line from the play."

"Hello, Mrs Tiggywinkle," I ventured. "This is baby Rufus."

"Louder," said the assistant. "And don't forget to refer to Rufus in the pram."

I had quite forgotten that I was supposed to be pushing a pram with a baby fox inside, probably because I couldn't see it. I repeated the line, directing my head downwards.

"It just sounds like a grunt," said the artistic director. "Can you speak up a little more?"

The inside of the mask was like a furnace by now.

"Hello, Mrs..." I yelled.

"Still too soft."

I was rapidly going off the idea of being Mrs Foxy but tried to press on. Think of what the Man in the Iron Mask went through, I told myself, but it was no good. All I wanted to do was get the flaming thing off as soon as possible and fumbled in vain for the fastening. Panic set in when I lost the eyehole and was plunged back into the suffocating darkness. Abandoning the toy fox cub in its pram, Basil Brush joined the cast of *Thriller* as I stumbled blindly towards my now unlikely employers, pointing to the mask in a frantic bid for assistance, hoping against hope that they hadn't gone to tea.

"I'm not sure this is for me," I told them after they had jointly and unceremoniously yanked the mask from my head.

"Perhaps not," agreed the artistic director, checking down the list for the next attendee.

I made for the door with as much dignity as I could muster, my hair stuck to my face in a sweaty mass, and the elusive Equity card even further out of reach.

With Jean Marlow in 'Daughters of Venice'

With Eamonn Jones in 'The Secret Garden'

The Man in Black

A Warning to the Curious was the title given by Mervyn, our director to an evening of supernatural tales at a stately home in Northamptonshire. Set around the time of Halloween to create a suitably spooky backdrop and with Mervyn, a diminutive character obsessed with Victorian gothic sweeping about in a long black cloak, the show seemed a guaranteed success. The action began with us actors gathered in a circle wearing hooded cloaks and holding torches under our chins while Mervyn introduced the proceedings.

"Ghosts," he hissed eerily. "What are they?"

'Don't know' quipped one of the actors quietly. This set us all sniggering and turned the evening of spine tingling tales into one of complete tomfoolery.

Mervyn then went on to quote the poem...

"From ghoulies and ghosties
And long-leggedy beasties
And things that go…

(There was meant to be a thud here on the sound tape Mervyn had made, like something falling to the floor or a heavy footstep on a stair, but it didn't happen so he just said the word 'bump').

in the night,
Good Lord, deliver us!"

Because of the delay waiting for the 'bump', it looked to the audience as though Mervyn had forgotten his lines. We all saw the funny side and our torches began to wobble even more.

We started off with a scene from Henry James' *The Turn of the Screw*. I played a governess sent to a remote country mansion to look after two weird children possessed by the evil Peter Quint. The governess encounters Quint (played by Mervyn himself), when she returns to the house having forgotten her gloves for church. Luckily I was wearing a bonnet which hid my expression in this scene as the missing 'bump' arrived at last, coinciding with Mervyn's appearance at the 'window' with a threatening "Haaaahhhhhhhh!" as he splayed his fingers menacingly.

The Room in the Tower by E.F. Benson tells of a young man who has nightmares about a room, (yes in a tower) occupied by a mysterious woman. On a visit to a friend he is given an identical room (yes, in a tower), and it's not long before the woman, who turns out to be a vampire, comes to claim him. Mercifully, I was not cast as the vampire who had to swoop down and 'bite' Mervyn's neck as it might have resulted in another corpse in addition to the one supposedly left drained on the bed.

The next tale, penned by Mervyn himself, was about a mysterious woman who in an act of revenge gets a waitress to throw herself from the roof of a department store. Mervyn explained that the woman is not of this world but from somewhere quite 'other' as no trace of her can be found after the deed has been done. The atmosphere was tense when as 'the woman', I lured the waitress into an alcove which served as the lift. Mervyn, who played the part of a customer in the store's café was seated at a nearby table. When he ordered "a pot of tea and a plate of fancies" in a cockney accent reminiscent of the late Irene Handl, I managed to remain straight-faced but it wasn't easy. It was Mervyn's sheer dedication and earnestness that I found so ticklish. Lord knows why, when it was the very thing that I myself should have been aspiring to.

The evening was rounded off by the scene from that old favourite, *A Christmas Carol* in which Scrooge is visited by his erstwhile business partner, Jacob Marley. To give him his due, Mervyn did a very good job as Scrooge, blaming Marley's appearance on indigestion. "You may be an undigested bit of beef, a blot of mustard, a crumb of cheese, a fragment of underdone potato," he exclaimed rolling his r's all Alistair Sim. "There's more of gravy than of grave about you, whatever you are!"

The show ended to resounding applause. It had been a long evening of haunting, but the ghosts had the last laugh. We arrived at the lodgings supposedly arranged by Mervyn only to discover that as with Marley and company, they didn't actually exist.

Mervyn assured us that his friend had promised to leave the back door key under a flower pot. After much skulking around and turning over of pots while we all stood shivering in the moonlight, Mervyn had to admit that something might have gone slightly wrong and went off to make a phone call. It had started to rain and we watched from the shelter of my car as he, a solitary cloaked figure in the village phone box, dialled to no avail. Mervyn's mate had obviously thought twice about loaning his property to strangers for the night, let alone a bunch of actors led by Mervyn.

Our earlier good humour having been replaced by dejection, fatigue and not least, hunger, I suggested we make the hour long journey to my house. On arrival, Mervyn's sinister 'Jack The Ripper' look was quickly replaced with a pair of stripy pyjamas and he sloped off to bed. The rest of us stuffed cheese on toast, turning over the events of the evening, not altogether kindly I'm afraid. The trouble is the creative mind isn't always an organised one and poor Mervyn, preoccupied with ghosts and gothic hadn't really got his act together as far we 'starving' actors were concerned. I think it's fair to say that unlike Marley, there was definitely more grave than gravy about him.

A Warning!

'The Alberts' were a musical comedy troupe that started out in the 1950s. Headed up by brothers, Tony and Dougie Gray, they appeared on television with Spike Milligan and at Peter Cook's Establishment Club in London. In the early 60s they put together an act of sheer mayhem involving a series of crazy sketches, songs and the playing of various instruments with just about anything occurring in between.

The Alberts were a major influence on the 'Bonzo Dog Doo-Dah Band', whose lead vocalist was Vivian Stanshall. In 1963 they presented *An Evening of British Rubbish* at the London Palladium attended by Princess Margaret.

It was while performing as a children's entertainer at a party for a one of their relatives that I was introduced to the Grays. Shortly after, on a balmy (or rather 'barmy') summer evening, I found myself at RAF Catterick, about to assist in a revival of The Alberts madcap show.

We didn't have much in the way of a rehearsal, just a brief run through at the Grays' rambling old home in Norfolk. We were supposed to go over everything on arrival at Catterick, including the use of props, many of which had rotted since their last outing. The afternoon evaporated and we were told to vacate the Officers' Mess in order for the tables to be set up for dinner. We were clearly in a mess of our own with no clear strategy yet in place for the show. All too soon the officers, having reached the brandy and cigars stage, were baying for the entertainment like an audience in ancient Rome.

Going by what I'd seen of a very poor quality video, one sketch of the Alberts' stage performance involved a couple of characters with a boat strapped to their shoulders to give the impression that they were on board. They'd tip over and spray each other with water from squeezy bottles to create the dubious illusion of a shipwreck. Among the troupe was the very talented Jeremy Minnis, known in East Anglia as the much loved children's entertainer, 'Oodly Doodly the Fenland Fool'. It was with Jeremy that I did the boat scene. The trouble was that we only had one squeezy bottle between us and therefore had to take it in turns to spray. This destroyed much of the spontaneity and provoked a 'boo' from those assembled.

Next was a hunting scene involving a person dressed as a rabbit being pursued by another with a shotgun. A picture rotating on a drum was supposed to create the illusion of the countryside flying by. Unfortunately, the rabbit costume was one of the many items that had gone missing. The shotgun wasn't in evidence either, so we were left with two people running along in the countryside. The backdrop eventually slipped down from its support, leaving the two people running on the spot for no apparent reason. Another boo ensued.

One of the Gray brothers, dressed as a woman, began an operatic aria. He then handed me the Italian verse, inviting me to take over. I couldn't begin to make out the words, which were in faint pencil, let alone sing them. Stage explosives having grown damp in their box over the years failed to produce the sound of dynamite at the designated time after a 'detonator' was pushed. As with Mervyn's 'bump', a loud impromptu blast occurred much later, during an entirely different sketch making everyone jump out of their skins.

The only part of the proceedings which we had managed to rehearse to any degree was a sketch based on a fellow picking up a prostitute and paying her to clamber up onto a wardrobe for some reason best known to the Alberts. Once she was safely up there, the joke was supposed to be that the punter would nick her handbag containing the night's takings before legging it out the door. In a short skirt and fishnets, I duly loitered until one of the brothers sauntered up and propositioned me. I swiped him several times with my handbag until he produced the correct amount of dosh. Only then did I allow him to follow me 'back to my place'.

Whereas the wardrobe we had used in Norfolk was quite substantial, the one brought for the show was nothing more than a tall rickety old cupboard. I managed to scramble up with the aid of a chair while the cupboard wobbled precariously. Once on top with my fishnets snagged to bits and my heart in my mouth, I reacted with appropriate hysterics. Not because my bag had been 'pinched', but out of genuine fear that the cupboard would topple over, pitching me into the lap of some unsuspecting officer and gentleman. (Richard Gere however was nowhere in sight).

Mercifully, a sketch involving someone being fired out of a cannon to the tune of *Fly Me To The Moon* had been omitted, but only due to transportation difficulties or I could have been heading, if not skywards, at least towards the back of the room in a puff of smoke with a pair of charred feet and my hair on end.

The audience weren't very generous for some reason (in fact they seem a bit fed up) and what brief ripple of applause that followed the show was probably due to relief that it was over.

Joking aside, looking back on that evening, I feel privileged to have worked with the Alberts and the now late Jeremy Minnis. The act might have gone down like the Titanic, but it was certainly a night to remember.

'Alberts' Dougie and Tony Gray (second and third from left) during the run of 'An Evening of British Rubbish' at the Comedy Theatre, London in 1963
(Copyright of the Lewis Morley Archive / National Portrait Gallery, London)

151

The Understudy

Abra-cadaver! at Windsor Theatre Royal with special effects by Ali Bongo, was a murder mystery in which I was understudying the female lead. American actor Frank Langella starred as a magician whose assistant got charred to death when a trick involving a giant cauldron went horribly wrong. They were using a shop mannequin for the 'body' which would tumble out stiffly from the 'flames' when the door flew open. I had offered my services in the cauldron to give some reality to the scene, but it was felt that the curtain would come down before people would notice that the 'body' wasn't human.

The role of the 'baddie' was played by a dwarf who in one scene locked the leading man inside a specially constructed metal cage, leaving a bunch of keys just beyond his reach. The show was set to go into the West End, but by sheer bad luck the backers arrived on an evening when several of the tricks went askew. The mannequin didn't even attempt to fall out of the cauldron (I did warn them) and during the scene with the dwarf the door to the cage fell wide open, leaving nothing to stop the 'imprisoned' actor from getting the keys. Sadly, the show closed after one week, but due to the nature of the contract I came away with a provisional Equity card. Abracadabra!

I understudied again on a tour of Alan Ayckbourn's *Absurd Person Singular*. It was paid work and I had a lot of fun touring the country for several weeks. Most evenings were spent playing cards in the dressing room with my fellow stand-ins. It was easy to get lulled into a sense of false security though, and one rainy afternoon I sauntered to the theatre in York to find that due to my actress being ill I was on for the matinee.

As wardrobe and make-up personnel began flitting around me I worried that the audience, disappointed at not seeing the billed actress might boo or ask for their money back. Also that the other cast members might be a bit unnerved by having me suddenly appear in their midst. The show went alright though with the only sound coming from the auditorium being that of sweet wrappers. Nevertheless, I was quite relieved to hand the reigns back for the evening show. I never felt that the role was my own, only borrowed, which is one of the hazards of understudying of course. I admire the late Jane Comfort who understudied the role of Mrs Boyle in *The Mousetrap* for ten years, starting when she was seventy-three. Apparently she did get to go on around sixty times though. There's a Sticker for you.

A Dangerous End

My morale was at an all time low when I was offered a major role — not the sort I'd been hoping for, but as permanent secretary to Alan, a busy accountant in Mayfair.

After years of no security and fly-by-nighting, the word 'permanent' was quite frightening. A true actor had to be flexible and prepared to drop everything when a job came up. However, penury was beginning to take its toll and I signed on the dotted line.

Alan was the nearest thing to a male version of Miranda Priestly, Meryl Streep's character in *The Devil Wears Prada*. He would start the day with a list of instructions and only wanted to hear from me once they had been carried out. I was never to ask questions. Every morning, instead of dumping a bag and coat on my desk á la Miranda, Alan would throw his car keys to me so that I could go and park his Rolls Royce. The first time I had to negotiate the spiral in Selfridge's garage, my heart was in my mouth. One scratch and I'd be history.

One wintry day, Alan informed me after launching the keys in my general direction that the car was out of petrol and had ground to a halt a few yards up the street.

"I only just made it here!" he announced as though I should feel sorry that he hadn't had the presence of mind to glance at the petrol gauge before leaving home. When I asked how I should go about the refuelling he suggested I head to Selfridges garage, purchase a petrol can and get it filled. "Bob's your uncle," he said with a wink.

Half an hour later, wearing an A-line coat in a force nine gale, I battled with the awkward petrol cap and the pouring in of the fuel without getting any on my person. A stray match from a passing smoker would have sent me up like the Hindenburg.

"Knew you could do it," said Alan with a grin as I handed back the keys, my face frozen, hair on end.

Alan didn't believe in paying for anything without putting up a fight. This included his household bills which were always left until the red final demands came in. He would often claim 'hardship' as the reason for late payment, although with a mansion on the outskirts of London he wasn't exactly living on the bread line. I was always returning broken toys to Selfridges and asking for refunds as, according to Alan, they must have been faultily manufactured. The acting training came in useful when I had to fend off creditors who, having despaired of reaching Alan by phone, would appear in reception. Alan was never to be found of course, always having foreseen their imminent arrival.

Typically, not long after joining Alan, I got that long awaited phone call from the Royal Shakespeare Company, inviting me to audition the following day.

The role was Emily, the courtesan in *Dangerous Liaisons* and to understudy the role of 'Madame de Tourvel' made famous on stage by Juliet Stevenson and on film by Michelle Pfeiffer.

The phones were ringing, Alan was waiting to dictate some urgent correspondence and I was sitting in the loo cramming my audition piece – 'Lady Macbeth' (Great-Auntie May didn't have this problem). Getting out for a couple of hours was a feat in itself but I was determined to do so.

When I arrived, sweaty and stressed out, I tried to focus on the business in hand. The director was fractious, having seen a constant stream of hopefuls all morning. The bright stage light dazzled me so I stepped out of it momentarily.

"The first rule of the stage of course is that the actor should find his light," said the director's assistant petulantly.

I felt like telling him to shut his face, but of course I was charm itself throughout what could possibly be a life-changing audition. Half way through *'Screw your courage to the sticking post and we'll not fail...'* it occurred to me that I'd forgotten to cancel Alan's lunch date and I did fail. The audition did prove to be life-changing in as much as I reached a decision. My stars were not in the ascendant it seemed. I'd never had a glimmer of real luck since starting out. My road to Damascus had become the road to nowhere. I would give up and resign myself to office life forever.

"What's up, doll?" asked Alan the following

morning. My failure of the previous day must've been all over my face.

"Nothing," I replied a little taken aback at Alan's concern.

"Good," he said pushing the car keys across my desk. "Off you go then."

Over at Selfridges' car park I felt like taking the Rolls Royce up to the roof and doing a *Thelma and Louise* off the top, only minus the 1966 green Thunderbird – well, minus Thelma and Louise really, just me in a big black Roller flying across the sky.

Freeze frame…

Of course I didn't really give up, but embarked on an additional creative outlet. I've been scribbling stories of one sort or another since I was a kid and decided to invest in some serious study. Over the years I've written various plays, short stories, and produced *Back Along the Track*, a childhood memoir about growing up in Ashford in the 60s. This gave me something to focus on when unfortunately, in 2008 my old (nameless) adversary decided to pay another visit. Again, I was brought back from the brink by a wonderful surgeon who I call 'Gandalf', as he has magic in his hands. Having had a section of bowel now removed (luckily there's quite a bit left, which comes in handy), I was beginning to feel like one of the characters in Kazuo Ishiguro's *Never Let Me Go,* who were bred for the purpose of donating their vital organs over a period of time. Unlike Keira Knightley and Carey Mulligan's characters in the film, I'm still here, although it's surprising that there's anything more than a little bit of skin, an eye and a tuft of hair left to tell the tale.

I did get to play in *Dangerous Liaisons* after all, at a theatre in Camden. I was cast as 'Madame de Volanges', mother of Cecily, a young girl seduced by the wicked 'Vicomte de Valmont'. This role was made famous on the stage by Alan Rickman and on the film by John Malkovich. (The next role for me will probably be Valmont's aunt, Madame de Rosamond who is in her eighties, should I still have my faculties.)

While I was appearing as Volanges the railway had its revenge for that fateful night years before, when I starred in my own one-off feature, *Trainstopping*. The train I was on broke down for three hours. I ended up forty minutes late for the show, having spent the afternoon in a cold sweat. Once we were on the move again, I dived into the train loo to get into my costume to save time. Mercifully, we could not afford the sumptuous eighteenth century style costumes and were performing in modern dress. (Likewise, it's a good thing it wasn't panto, as to emerge from the toilet dressed as Humpty Dumpty would have been less than cool.)

Luckily, the rest of the cast were lovely and forgiving. The play went well despite the late start, which as Valmont would have put it was 'Beyond my control'.

Where was I? Oh, yes…After branching into screenwriting, I wrote the plots for several short films, trying ideas out on my long suffering family. Whereas I once had my sisters dressing up in the back garden at Twelve Acres all those years ago, it was their kids who starred in my mini epics.

I wrote and appeared in *Leonora*, a 'scary' short film about contacting someone from the 'other side' with the help of an Ouija board (it could happen!). This was directed by the excellent Tom Hooker who has since gone on to do brilliant things. More recently, I wrote and co-produced a short thriller entitled *Foolproof*, which was directed by the fabulous award-winning director, Trevor Hughes. I'm currently writing further episodes of *Tower Street*, a soap which has been shown at lunch times in the West End and will appear on the web in 2013.

I've tried to remain positive throughout my life about whatever has been thrown at me. I don't ever dwell on having been ill, but it did put things into perspective. I would like to have been able to 'give up the day job', but if the last twenty-five years has taught me anything it's that there's more to life than waiting for 'the phone call'.

As someone once said 'It is better to journey than to arrive.' It's the friendships, the experiences good and bad along the way that count.

Besides, who wants to be famous anyway? Jetting around the world, being invited to glitzy events, having lots of money and being offered wonderful parts. Yeah, who needs it?

Hang on a minute…Was that my phone…?

With Tom Hooker, the cast and crew of 'Leonora'

With my nieces and nephews 'on location'

162

Solving a 'mystery' at Willesborough Mill

The kids would often make creative suggestions

Making 'Foolproof',
with actress Jo Hart

Acknowledgements

With thanks to Angela, Sharon, Michelle,
Graham and Richard.

To Sandie for the photographs of schooldays.

To nurses and school chums I couldn't trace to
thank personally.

To Ian and all my family for sharing my universe
(including the black holes).